To Chuck & Kathy
Hi-de-ho neighbors.
Retire well & prosper.

Darrell

A Hope in Hell

By

Darrell Keifer

D1559634

A Hope in Hell
Copyright © 2019 by Darrell Keifer

Books>science fiction>thriller>apocalypse>eco-fiction>dark humor

ISBN: 9781796695083

Editor: Ann N. Videan, ANVidean.com

Cover by Ivan, bookcoversart.com

Dedication

To the survivors of Lake Nyos

TABLE OF CONTENTS

Chapter I

Hamlet's Ghost

Jason Adams cupped his hands and peered through the glass separating Neonatal and the rest of the world. On one side, swaddled in pink or blue blankets, lay new life—the product of meiosis, sexual union, and gestation—on the other, the mortal world of mitosis fated for maturation, degeneration, and death. At forty-five, Jason stood well past the maturation stage on the mitosis side.

Fourteen newborns in fourteen basinets lay queued up to the window. One nurse changed a diaper while another picked up a pink-draped baby and presented her for viewing. A father beamed, waved, and cooed through the glass. The nurse returned the baby and pointed at Jason as if to ask, "Which one is yours?"

Jason shook his head and stepped back. The father looked at him.

"We're. . . ahh. . . just thinking about it." Jason smiled and turned away.

He marched back through the maze of Seattle's Sisters of Mercy Hospital corridors and across the sky bridge to his usual haunts in the professional building. As a psychologist, he occasionally took a break from other people's problems, strolled down to the Neonatal Unit and warmed his heart in the baths of renewal and hope. Sometimes that worked, but sometimes it just filled him with longing. This was one of the latter "sometimes." His wife wasn't getting any younger and neither was he, but every time he broached the subject of having a family, she put it off and changed the topic.

Jason entered his one-man office. Though he sometimes volunteered at the hospital, he did contract work for the Department of Family Services (DFS). Through DFS, he dealt with a lot of teenagers. Many had lost a parent, or parents, or had become estranged from them for one reason or another. He could do only the minimums—put Band-Aids on wounds that needed stitches. DFS budgets had been reduced every year for the last decade. As a contract psychologist, his complaints were seconded by bureaucrats, but eventually fell on the deaf ears of politicians.

When Jason opened the file of his last appointment, darkness already loomed outside his window. Though the days slowly grew longer, the February sunset came way too early. This last case involved a young man recently out of prison and still on probation. Jason tried to avoid it, arguing the case should be sent to the Department of Corrections, but they were as overloaded as DFS.

Tyrell Jones looked the part; his eyes shifted suspiciously around the room as he entered, tattoos covered his arms and neck, and he plunked down with enough force to show attitude. Jason bit his lip, *correction officers are better equipped to handle this*, but he put on his nonplussed expression.

"Tyrell, I'm Dr. Adams. What can I help you with?"

The young man continued looking around the office. "I don't know. My probation officer sent me here."

Jason knew that wasn't true. They only sent people who had requested help, but he decided not to directly challenge the young man.

"Your profile says you were married and stayed married while you were in prison."

Tyrell fixed upon a framed cartoon displayed on Jason's desk. "What's that?"

The cartoon showed an anxious man in a grocery store facing hundreds of yogurt choices with the caption, *"Where's my Xanex?"* Jason pointed to it with his thumb. "It's an example of the paradox-of-choice. It's, ah . . . an inter-office joke."

"You the only one here."

"The joke's on me." Jason picked up the display and looked at it. "I took care of my Mom who was sick for a long time. So, when she passed away I suddenly had a great deal of freedom. But, I had a hard time making decisions about my life, about what I wanted. It's called the Hamlet Syndrome."

"Well, I ain't ever had that problem. I just can't sleep right now. All the things I was gonna do when I got out, don't mean nothin' no more. Maybe I need sleepin' pills or somethin'."

"It says here your wife died of cancer almost a year ago, and you weren't allowed to attend the funeral. That had to be hard."

"That's history. I don't wanna talk about my dead wife." Tyrell grimaced.

Jason tapped his fingers on the desk. "Tyrell, if we haven't grieved, sometimes we hold—"

Bam! Tyrell had jumped up and slammed the desk.

Jason flinched and ducked his head. His eyes fixed on a tattoo of a horned snake on the back of the young man's right fist.

Tyrell bawled, "I'm outta prison, now. Nothin' else matters. You gonna give me somethin' or not?"

When his gaze fell on Jason, who nearly curled into a ball, Tyrell's eyes widened, and he stepped back. As fast as he had exploded, he sat down. "I'm sorry, dude. Please don't tell my probbie."

Jason gathered himself, disappointed at his own reaction. He took a couple of deep breaths, and reached over and tapped something on his glass desktop.

"Hamlet, file JM 16." A hologram appeared above his desk. "Sometimes I work over at the hospital. Tell me the first thing that comes to mind."

An image formed—a boy in a hospital bed, leg missing, bandaged, face scarred. Tyrell frowned.

"First thought. Quickly, now," Jason demanded.

"He's been hurt," Tyrell intoned as if he had been asked the sum of two plus two.

"He's ten. Car accident."

Jason clicked to the next image—a child, head shaved, hospital gown and oxygen tube, skin and bones. Jason nodded toward Tyrell.

"I, ah . . . looks like leukemia or somethin'."

"Yes. Diagnosed only a month ago." Jason continued, "I suspect you've never properly grieved for your wife. You've held it inside."

The next hologram showed an adult burn victim—changing of the bandages.

Jason looked up. "But, at some point, Tyrell, grief just becomes self-pity."

"What are you tryin' ta do? Stop it!" Tyrell looked away, but his gaze drifted back to the image. "What's that?"

"The ol' burn unit. Usually takes a couple hours to change the bandages. They say it's worse than . . . than almost anything." Jason flipped through several holograms of burn patients. "Some want to rip them off quickly, others go slow."

Another image of a man and woman sitting in a waiting room.

"They look like those people in the ghetto."

Jason cocked his head. "Why?"

Tyrell pointed. "They whipped. Given up. You can see it in dey faces."

"Good read. Their son underwent brain surgery for a tumor. He didn't make it."

Next, a paraplegic fitting a prosthesis.

"Enough." Tyrell's voice rose an octave. "I know what you're trying to do." He hung his head in silence. Eventually, a sob escaped his throat. "It shoulda been me. She was the good one. Darla suffered. Had a lot of pain. She was so doped up on morphine I couldn't talk to her on the phone, and I couldn't be with her."

He buried his head in his hands and cried. A few moments passed before Tyrell regained control.

"You said self-pity. You think I'm just wallowin' in my own pity party."

"I'm saying once we've grieved, we can move on. It's not that we ever forget those we loved. The pain will never go away, but if we never find anything greater than ourselves, it becomes just that—a pity party." Jason sat down. "If Darla were able to talk to you right now, what would she say?"

Tyrell kept his gaze down, thought a moment, and shook his head. "I don't know."

"Let's reverse roles. You just died of cancer and she's alive. What would you say to Darla?

Tyrell took several deep breaths. "Ta get on with her life."

Jason touched his nose and pointed. "Now, you know."

Tyrell's shoulders relaxed. He looked at the psychologist and murmured, "I get it. Yeah." Sitting up straight he released a deep breath. "Yeah. I think you're right." The young man's gaze turned toward the exit. "I can quit this anytime, can't I?"

"Depends on whether you can sleep or not."

Tyrell nodded. "We'll see."

Jason pulled a sheet of paper from his desk, leaned over and passed it to the young man. "A grief therapy group meets every week at the hospital. This might be a good step for you."

Tyrell shrugged, stood, walked to the door and looked back. "You can't tell anybody about this, right."

"I am legally bound to a code of silence."

"Thanks, man." Tyrell made eye contact and shut the door behind him.

Jason sat down and spoke deliberately. "Prince Hamlet, file entry. Tyrell Jones."

Dong. The toll of a distant bell. A computer-generated hologram of Hamlet, dressed in fifteenth century garb and holding a quill, appeared above his desk. "My good lord, shalt this be an open file?" asked the ancient Dane.

"No, this will be closed."

The document displayed an image of Tyrell. Jason leaned back. "Date, time." The date filled in—February 27th, 2029, 6:00 p.m. "First session, the client has begun the grieving process, but only started to move from anger to acceptance. Judging from his eyes and pallor, he's using alcohol and possibly other depressants. That may trigger his depression. He requested a sleeping aid and expressed anger when I redirected the conversation. My own version of the Jacobson-Meyer compassion test seemed engaging, and he showed some ability for self-reflection. I recommended he attend a grief support group. It may help move him toward the next stage. End entry."

"So be it, m'lord."

Jason stood, stretched. "Hamlet, call my wife."

"Yes, sire."

Jason stepped around his desk, sat on the floor and assumed a yoga position.

"Fie, my honorable lord, fie. She doth not answer."

"Where the hell's my wife?" Jason muttered to himself. "Damn it. She's always busy."

"Shall I continue to summon?"

Jason stretched up from a downward dog to a sun salutation. "No. ''Tis an unweeded garden that grows no seed.'"

"Shall I look up gardening?"

"I don't think that would help." Jason sank down into a child's pose. "What time does the Bioneer's Conference start tonight?"

"The keynote presentation initiates at seven bells."

Jason tapped his wrist impress to show the time. "Ahh, 'time is out of joint,' but they always start late." He bowed with a yogic salutation. "Namaste." He put his shoes on and grabbed a coat. "Good night, sweet prince. Activate the alarm system."

* * * * *

Elaina Adams held zero interest in the Bio . . . whatever conference. *Jason, always trying to save the world.* She turned her cell phone off and drove the Mercedes downtown to meet two friends at an after-work hot spot near the tech industry district. Elaina enjoyed their meetings, enjoyed speaking Russian again, and maybe . . . maybe vicariously enjoyed the interplay of sex, money, and envy as her Russian peers jockeyed for lifestyle and status.

She entered Finnegan's Study, an Irish upscale watering hole in Bellevue just east of Seattle in the heart of the high-tech district. Its compartmentalized over-hung alcoves, overstuffed chairs, and overpriced single malt Scotch attracted the wealthy, high-tech, Steve-Jobs-wannabe crowds. Elaina knew turning heads in a nerd bar was easy. She allowed the slightest one-sided upturned smile as she drew gazes, once-overs, and outright stares.

Most of these men, so young. Would they be interested if they knew I was thirty-eight? Hmm, of course they would.

Nadia's long arms, extending out of her sleeveless red dress, waved above the other customers.

When Elaina approached, Nadia bounced off her stool and ran over to hug her—a display as much for the men watching as for Elaina.

"Come, my friend. I've much to tell you."

Elaina slid onto a stool across from Tina. "*Privet. Radt tobya videt, Tina.*"

"You've had your hair done, I love the bangs, you look so beautiful." Tina reached over and flipped her fingers through her friend's long tresses.

Nadia put her arm around Elaina. "Vee are celebrating. You must help us." She reached for three of several brimming shot glasses and pushed them toward her. "You've got to catch up." Nadia giggled. "Stoli, good Russian vodka. *Vashe zdorovie!* Ha ha."

Elaina smiled. "What are we celebrating?"

"Tina is getting divorce!" Nadia lifted her glass high.

Tina stood and joined her. "*Za dam.* To women! To women!"

Elaina took up her glass. "To women."

Seeing the girls down their shots, several nearby men jokingly took up the toast.

"To women."

"To divorced women."

The friends ignored the chatter and sat again. Elaina leaned over to Tina. "So, everything all right? What about immigration?"

"Hell with immigration! Has been two years. I am American citizen. They cannot touch me," Tina spouted.

Elaina frowned. *Did the marriage turn sour, or was this planned from the beginning?* "What are you going to do? How will you live?"

A Hope in Hell

Nadia leaned in. "Tina's lawyer says the prenuptial is not enforceable. She gets half—"

Tina waggled her feet like a little girl. "I rich, I rich. I free, I free." She hoisted another shot of vodka and drained it. "Hooray!"

Elaina sipped at hers. "What about Paul?"

"To hell with Paul. Men! They think through their—" Tina pointed downward.

"Penises!" Tina and Nadia yelled together.

Tina scanned the table for another drink. "Vodka, we need vodka."

Almost on cue, a waiter arrived with three more shots. Elaina reached for her purse, but the waiter held up his hand and pointed. "From the gentlemen at table six, in the alcove behind you."

They took up the drinks and turned to the alcove. Three young men, about the same age as Tina, raised their glasses. Nadia and Tina downed their shots, but Elaina only touched the vodka to her lips.

"Slow down, Tina. You are going to get drunk."

"We are Russian women. We can drink like Cossacks." Tina reached over, pushing Elaina's glass up to her lips. "We celebrate." She burped, giggled. "I am going to thank those *detishki*."

She rose and walked over to the alcove. As the men stood to welcome her, Tina threw her arms around the first one, held his head, and kissed him on each cheek in a traditional Russian greeting. Elaina and Nadia laughed.

Elaina turned to Nadia. "And, you. How are you and Richard?"

Hamlet's Ghost

"Fine. Boring." Nadia tapped her fingers. "And, you. Marry doctor, drive Mercedes, Nordstrom clothes. You happy?"

Elaina nodded. "Dr. Adams is a very nice man. We . . . we are happy." Elaina shook her head. "But, he wants a baby. Child."

Nadia turned to watch Tina laughing and flirting with the three young men.

Nadia laughed. "Come, let us join them."

* * * * *

Jason timed his arrival just right, the attendees had been welcomed, the sponsors thanked, and the platitudes given. The tiered auditorium held more than six hundred patrons—a mix of shirt-and-tie engineers, turtlenecked biologists, tee-shirted hippies, greenies, and students. He took an aisle seat in the back behind two men, one older and one younger. The younger man whispered something to his associate—he seemed to be translating in French as the headline speaker, Dr. Lamar, took the podium.

> "If you are a human being, living upon the surface of the Earth today, you should bend down and give this planet a hug because, as a species, you had the perfect birthday. *Homo sapiens sapiens* evolved at the perfect geologic time, a time of incredible stability. We haven't had any comet strikes ending seventy-five percent of life on Earth in the last sixty-five million years, no geo-scale

11

volcanic activity to choke us or sear our lungs, and no scorching celestial love embrace from a solar hiccup. So, we live by grace, by the grace of astronomy, by the grace of geology."

The older man in front of Jason became very animated and turned to the younger one. "*GRACE*, he said *GRACE*."

"*Non, non, non. Pas du tout . . . grace an Anglais word. Non.*" The younger man reassured the Frenchman, who returned to the speaker with an intense scrutiny.

". . . in terms of biodiversity. Again, our species was designed, beta tested, built, and shipped when the Earth's biosphere peaked in diversity. The late Precambrian may have boasted only a few hundred thousand species. Even the Cambrian explosion increased to only two or three million. But, our time, the Holocene, the age of humans, an estimated eight million species exist today. From single cell organisms to termites that build architectural wonders, from mayflies that live a day to tortoises that live over two hundred years, from cyanobacteria that poison our waterways to algae that produce biofuels, we live in a veritable Garden of Eden."

Hamlet's Ghost

Jason couldn't help but be distracted by the ongoing translation in front of him. He hadn't taken French since high school. He leaned back away from the men and refocused on the presentation.

> ". . . species already undergoing anthropogenic mass extinction. Tortoises produce an enzyme, telomerase, that promotes better replication during mitosis. Wouldn't it be nice to learn how that enables them to live so long, before they become extinct?"

Jason picked out a few phrases of the French conversation: "*An accident . . . he knows nothing. It's not public yet.*"

> ". . . So, sessions on Biomimicry, Pascal's Wager and Climate Change, Passive Engineering and Home Energy Efficiency, Today's Geo Engineering Efforts, Lake Nyos and Ocean Currents, and the latest in Solar Energy and Wind Technology. Enjoy the sessions."

The crowd applauded, rose, and exited to the individual seminars.

Jason leaned forward. "*Excusez-moi. Ahh*. You seemed concerned about the sessions?"

The Frenchmen gave each other conspiratorial glances. "No, no, no. This is Doctor Jean Girard. He is an oceanographer and is giving one of the seminars." The young man looked at the doctor, who ever-so-slightly shook his head. "Concern . . . ahh, no just some data not yet published, proprietary, is all."

The two stood and stepped into the aisle, the older man leading the way, then the young man suddenly turned back, his expression inexplicably bleak. "'Lake Nyos and Ocean Currents.' You should come."

Jason followed the crowds to the conference board and found the room for the Lake Nyos talk. He'd heard of Lake Nyos before, but couldn't remember where. By the time Jason got there, Dr. Girard had already started. The wall behind him showed an image of a valley strewn with dead cattle.

"Lake Nyos in the mountains of Cameroon, Africa, is a deep crater lake within the Oku volcano field. Volcanic release of gases under the lake's thermocline led to a buildup of carbon dioxide. The lake stored the gases, like a carbon gun, then suddenly released . . . *une explosion*."

Dr. Girard looked at his interpreter.

"A sudden turnover."

"With an explosive turnover, in 1986. These photos were taken by investigators the next day."

Another image along the lake shore: washed up dead fish, birds, dogs.

"The gases were mostly carbon dioxide, hydrogen sulfide, only traces of caustic gases."

Dr. Girard clicked the next image: Several bodies lay scattered about a village. "Most of the villagers died in their homes."

Click. Hut's interior, a family lay dead, mouths agape.

Click. More interiors.

Hamlet's Ghost

The audience let out a few startled gasps.

"There were three villages in the valley, seventeen-hundred people died. Though there was some caustic injury, the cause of death was a combination of hypoxia and hypercapnia. The percent of volcanic gases lowered the oxygen partial pressure at the same time high carbon dioxide caused what miners call 'blackdamp.' We normally, in the air, *aspirons* twenty-one percent oxygen, but *nous sommes fragiles.*"

Girard again looked to the young man.

"We breathe twenty-one percent oxygen."

"But, we are fragile. Lower that percentage to sixteen percent and we struggle, we breathe harder, but the CO_2 in the blood will still stay too high. Simply increasing the CO_2 concentration by one percent causes drowsiness; three percent, headaches and impaired mental function, five to ten percent, blackout and death."

Click. Another overhead view of the valley, looking like the post-apocalypse.

"If we extract from this, we can take the ratio of the mass of the heavier-than-air gases, 300,000 tons, to the size of the valley and apply it to the ocean's 'stored' gases. The 530,000 gigatonnes of clathrates on the continental shelves, and the 660 gigatonnes of dissolved organic matter in the deep ocean sinks, provide enough mass to create the same carbon-gun scenario."

A few in the crowd let out audible groans.

An older man stood and interrupted, "I'm an oceanographer with the U.S. Geophysics Institute. You said same scenario? For what, Pacific islands, the coastal communities?"

Dr. Girard looked at his young interpreter. "*Non, le monde*, the world."

The audience exhaled a collective gasp, and began chattering.

Dr. Girard held up a silencing palm toward the crowd. "Of course, this is theoretical." The crowd quieted. "Ocean currents are still stable, the methane clathrates, are, ahh . . ."

The interpreter added, "The clathrates are in a delicate balance of temperature and pressure."

". . . and should stay in its semi-solid state," Girard finished.

A woman sitting next to Jason whispered, "Are you a scientist? Do you understand what he's covering?"

"Sorry, I'm a psychologist. I'm as lost as most people." Jason paused, and then decided to add, "But, watch his body language. Look there, they did it again."

The woman shook her head. "Did what?"

"They keep looking at each other. They're nervous, they're hiding something."

A young man raised a hand. "What of NASA's GRACE II mission anomalies? How does that—"

Several people in the crowd piped up. "No tech-speak, please."

The young man continued, "GRACE II is Gravity Recovery and Climate Experiment. Satellites track variations in gravity that can reveal small changes in deep ocean currents. Recently there has been a change in the South Pacific."

Jason perked up, remembering the French doctor's previous reaction to the use of the word "grace." This time Dr. Girard walked over to his interpreter, held a hand up, and whispered something.

The interpreter nodded. He turned to the audience, gestured broadly, and gave an unconvincing but dismissive summary. "Of course, we are working with the U.S. in analyzing the data. But, I'm afraid we are out of time."

Many audience members sighed and looked at their watches. There was still session time left.

Jason attended another seminar on renewable energy and then called Elaina. Again, no response. Tired after a long week, he decided to go home. He'd sleep-in tomorrow and return for more conference sessions on Saturday afternoon.

* * * * *

Elaina stood alone at the standup bar. She thought about joining her friends, but knew what that could lead to. She decided to finish her vodka and leave. She looked over at Tina and Nadia who were smiling and laughing and changed her mind. She drained the shot glass, grabbed her purse, and did a fashion-model-catwalk saunter over to the alcove.

Warm greetings, serotonin boosting drugs, and plentiful shots worked their way into her cerebral cortex. Images became disjointed, sensations became pleasurable, and even casual contact became sensual.

Elaina sat in the back seat of an SUV; the party was moving to a Queen Anne townhouse. One of the young men who sat in the center, kissed Nadia, then turned to kiss her. Playful, gratifying. More drugs, more vodka—Elaina's inhibitions melted like spilt ice cream on a summer sidewalk—more kissing, more groping.

Chapter II

Slings and Arrows

Jason woke up less than refreshed. He stayed up late trying to phone his wife, but had received no response. By two in the morning he drifted off to sleep on the couch and didn't wake until seven. Shaking off his grogginess, he immediately walked to the garage to see if her Mercedes was there. It wasn't.

Jason made some kind of yuppie green tea, sat down at his breakfast nook, and gazed over the kitchen. The stainless steel refrigerator, double ovens, dishwasher, and black marble counter tops all seemed too cold and sterile, more appropriate for an autopsy room than a home. His gaze continued over to the generous dining room with its long cherry-wood table and twelve empty chairs. His wife had gushed over this when they went house shopping. He thought back to the tiny kitchen of his childhood. It's built in drop-down table could barely squeeze four chairs around it. *Why had it seemed so big?* He, his mother, and sister had shared that one-bedroom apartment, but it was so full of life.

He returned to his tea and stared out the window. Across the street on the greenbelt's manicured lawns, neighbors gathered for a Tai-Chi-On-the-Grass session. Sometimes Jason joined in, but not this morning. The usual cohort lined up in front of the instructor: a dozen mid-forties to mid-fifties housewives, one or two men of the same age, and the one bright spot in the mix—the lady with the two boys.

The two little boys frolicked on the adjacent playground. So well behaved, Jason thought. The instructor faced the rising sun, raised arms, deep breath, arms descended, palms down, exhaled—welcoming heaven to earth. The well-heeled participants mimicked the flow of arms, breath, and chi.

Noise from the front of the house caught his attention. The garage opened. Jason waited. The car door closed and footsteps entered the house. Elaina, carrying her purse, clothes a little rumpled, stalked straight down the hall, with a furtive glance to the kitchen.

"Oh!" Elaina startled, almost jumped. "Jason. You scared me. Sorry I did not call you. I got a little drunk and spent the night at Nadia's. Too much vodka."

Jason set his tea down. *She said that almost too fast.*

"I was worried about you. Your phone was off." He walked toward her and reached out his arms, but Elaina shrank back.

"I'm sorry, I'm dirty. I'm going to shower and sleep." She proceeded down the hall with her hand over the opening of her purse.

She feels guilty. "Wait. Was Richard there?"

"Yes . . . ahh, no he was gone somewhere."

"Elaina, what's going on? Don't you think I know when you're lying?"

"Nyet. Stop it. Don't analyze me. Save it for your patients." Elaina threw down her purse, her angry gaze challenged Jason, then cast downward.

"Let's talk." Jason pointed to the kitchen table. He walked over and sat down. Elaina stood with her arms crossed.

Finally, she strode over and scooted onto the counter-height stool, but kept her arms locked, her jaw set. "I want divorce!" She stared at the table top.

Jason sat straight and rigid. "You can't mean that. I want a family. Our family."

Elaina retorted, "You talk of this all the time. You have ideal dreamland. But, what of I want?" Her English became more broken as she became angrier.

Jason's face reddened. "I told you when we married, I'll wait till you're ready."

"For a psychologist, you are so *efuka* blind. Three years, I say no. I did not come here for citizenship. I came over here for you and this life. But, I don't want a family! We want different things."

Jason stood, his face pale, clammy. "We all need to find something other than ourselves. I need . . . we need. To fulfill our lives. To love something more than, than—"

Sweat beaded his forehead, he clutched his left arm, fell to the floor and hit his head.

"Jason. Jason! What is wrong? *'Tchyo za ga 'lima?*" Elaina rushed around the table, stooped down, and cradled Jason's head in her lap.

An elephant sat on Jason's chest. All he could do was witness his own heart attack.

Elaina scurried away but returned with her phone as Jason's world went dark.

* * * * *

21

A Hope in Hell

Jason awoke with a tube in his nose and a hell of a headache. Disoriented, it took a while to realize he lay in a hospital bed. He remembered the ache in his arm, the pain in his chest. *What happened?* He noticed the IV and tried to sit up, but a sharp pain along his ribs stopped him. Opening his shirt revealed red welts on his chest. Poking around, he found the source of the soreness lay beneath the welts. Broken rib? Painfully craning his neck, he groped for a call button and pushed it.

A nurse entered—short dark hair, mid-thirties, scrubs, her neck decorated with a gold locket. She gave an empathetic smile.

"All awake, I see, Mr. Adams. Hi, I'm Emily Bloom. How are you feeling? I'll check some vitals. The doctor is making the rounds now. He'll be here soon."

"Ackk." *Cough.* "Ackk." The soreness in his throat arrested his attempt to speak.

"Mr. Adams, don't try to talk. You've had a breathing tube down your throat. It's probably bruised a bit. Stage whisper only." She leaned close. "You know what a stage whisper is?"

Jason nodded and let out a whisky-throated affirmation. "I played Hamlet in college. Voice, do thy work. Now, where the hell am I?"

"Sense of humor, that's a good sign." Emily inclined her head. "You're at Mercy Providence. You have suffered a cardiac arrest, but that's about all I can tell you. The doctor will answer further questions." She took out a blood pressure cuff. "We're monitoring your blood pressure, but I'm going to double check."

"My wife?" Jason's eyes pleaded.

"She was here yesterday."

Jason grimaced. "We were fighting when . . ." He pointed to the monitor.

"I'm sure she'll be back."

Jason appreciated her empathetic optimism.

* * * * *

Jason pushed a button on the hospital bed lifting him to an upright position, the oxygen tube still taped under his nostrils.

Dr. Moorhead entered with digital tablet and stethoscope. He stood at the foot of the bed and began. "Dr. Adams, I'm afraid I have some bad news. Your tests show advanced ventricular cardiomyopathy. In the long term, you need a new heart. Unfortunately, your age doesn't place you at the top of the transplant list. There are few A-B negative donors. Statistically, matching blood type, Rh, Kell, etcetera, within the general population is only one in two thousand."

Jason had prepared himself for bad news, but this exceeded his worst-case-scenario. He sat in dumbfounded disbelief. *He's talking about me, about my life, as if it was a candle in the wind.*

"The heart is damaged. The meds you're taking should lower risk of a reoccurrence. We are going to keep you here for a day or so to monitor and see how you react to the drugs. Then you may go home, as long as you stay within a prescribed diet and rest regime."

Jason's vision narrowed, the doctor's words sounded as if coming through a tunnel. Jason remembered his training for relating bad news to clients—be deliberate, pause and listen, compare with others who are worse off, and offer some hope at the end. *Jason Adams, star of a psychiatric training film showing the stages of loss.* He knew he was in denial, knew his question was hopeless, but found his voice and asked it anyway. "Transplant? Alternatives: stents, valves, surgery?"

"I'm afraid cardiomyopathy like this, with a thickening of the heart muscle, has no other long-term treatment. The risk of a fatal heart attack is thirty percent within the first three months, fifty percent within six months, and ninety percent within a year. And, that's with blood thinners, and no outside stress in your life. We sit tight and wait for a donor."

Dr. Moorhead leaned forward, and spoke with all the compassion of a funeral director. "On the positive side, the paramedics got to you in time. They were able to resuscitate without any major stroke or loss of mental function. I do not recommend returning to work. Waiting is your job now."

Chapter III

The Gates of Hell

Susan Martin tweeted on her cell phone as their white panel van exited the freeway and wound along an isolated forested road toward the new experimental prison.

The driver, a grad-student intern, peered through the windshield. "Is this it? Seems . . ."

Susan glanced up. "Kinda spooky."

The architecture appeared out of place nestled in the softwood pine forests of northern California. The building's footprint belied its size with eight of its nine floors underground, extending down toward its namesake. Painted forest-brown, it could have been a typical government institutional building. A cinderblock wall topped with wrought iron pickets surrounded the structure. No guard towers, no concertina wire. The only giveaways as to the function of the simple austere rectangle were its few grated windows and lack of external amenities.

The entrance swung into view along with a dozen other vehicles parked outside the closed gates. *"HELL'S GATE—SEDATION INCARCERATION FACILITY,"* loomed over the steel-gated entrance.

"Yay, our peeps are here." Susan nodded toward a clump of people huddled in front of the wrought iron fencing. "And, I see a network camera crew. I told you 'The Prophet' would bring publicity."

"This guy murdered a lot of people. We won't get much public sympathy," the intern cautioned.

"We stay on message. Strictly a human rights issue."

As soon as the vehicle stopped, the two women bounced out of the van and opened the back doors to reveal a pile of protest signs.

Susan grabbed a bullhorn. "If you're here to protest judicial sedation as cruel and unusual punishment, come on over!"

Nearly thirty people queued up as the intern handed out signs.

Susan guided them to the gate and into a moving, human conveyor belt of posters and signboards.

"Judicial Sedation is Death"

"Deep Sleep is a Violation of Constitutional Rights"

"Cruel and Unusual, No Permanent Sleep."

As they circled, she led them in a chant, "Close Hell's Gate, Close Hell's Gate."

Susan passed the bullhorn to her intern. "Keep it moving. I want them in the background when I give an interview to the news cameras."

She approached the network correspondent, Martha Walker, and her camera crew. She spoke with Martha as a cameraman clipped a mic onto her lapel in preparation for the interview.

Suddenly, three red, white, and blue vans from Senatorial candidate Ted Stadum's campaign headquarters roared into the parking lot. Out poured workers and supporters dressed in campaign regalia. His staff set up a podium, passed out signs to a dozen supporters, and bunched them up behind the hastily raised dais.

The Gates of Hell

A black limousine rolled up. Stadum's press secretary, along with Stadum and his trophy wife, exited to the cheers cued up by his support staff.

"Oh, shit. That asshole," Susan muttered to herself.

Martha turned to her cameraman with a "get this," leaving Susan hanging out to dry.

Stadum took the podium. "I just heard the sentence for Reverend Branson, aka 'The Prophet' . . . ninety years judicial sleep. Like the ACLU," he gave a dismissive nod toward Susan, "I think that's not fair. The mass murdering reverend sent dozens of innocent people to the big sleep, and he gets to go to dreamland? I say the son-of-a-bitch deserves execution!"

His supporters cheered on cue.

"But, if we are not allowed to carry out true justice, judicial sedation is the next best thing. Incarceration costs you, the tax payer, four hundred dollars a day. More than most people make. But, sleep is cheap. Sedation costs less than forty dollars a day. Ask yourself, what do you prefer to pay for?"

Cheers.

"Vote Stadum, I support judicial sedation!"

Susan grimaced as the candidate's entourage swept into the limo and vanished as swiftly as it arrived. The correspondent waved to her cameraman and turned to go.

Susan stepped over. "Hey. Hey! Don't you want to hear the other side? We have legitimate constitutional issues here."

Martha looked at her cameraman and reluctantly nodded toward Susan.

"I am here with Susan Martin of the ACLU. She and a small group of supporters are protesting judicial sedation. Ms. Martin?"

"Nothing robs us more of our own humanity than the denial of humanity in others. By taking away the consciousness of a human being, we deny that person the ability to regret, to feel remorse, to seek forgiveness, to rehabilitate. We find that—"

"Ms. Martin, supporters of judicial sedation claim that traditional prison is the most violent environment in the world outside of war. And, given the high rate of recidivism, inmates are better off in sedation than in prison."

"I'm not denying our prison system is in need of reform. But, imagine a young man who robs a liquor store, gets twenty years judicial sleep, and wakes up a forty-some-year-old man. Robbed of his youth, robbed of life. No chance to—"

Martha glanced at her wrist readout. "Thank you, Ms. Martin. We got what we need." The interviewer motioned to the cameraman. "We've got to hustle to make the six o'clock." The newswoman and the cameraman scurried back to their vehicle.

Susan rolled her eyes and shook her head.

* * * * *

Warden Jeff Ramsey stood with his arms crossed, monitoring the protests outside. He watched through the lobby doors as the camera crews drove away, followed by the left-wing nut cases. The warden waved to the two guards he had

The Gates of Hell

posted in the gatehouse. They stood ready to keep people out, not to keep inmates in. Guards at his sleepy little kingdom were almost a redundancy. Ramsey turned and headed toward the induction room and his favorite part of the job—welcoming new guests. There would be no perp walk, damn courts wouldn't allow cameras, there would be no humiliated degenerates, no monsters caught in the harsh light of the law, but Jeff Ramsey would be there. He'd step in to bear witness and stand proxy for the Gods of Justice. Besides, the trio of new guests was infamous, and he had some fresh material to try out.

Three grim uniformed barbers awaited their next customers. Warden Ramsey nodded to one of the guards who opened a door and led three, shackled, orange-clad inmates into the chairs. Ramsey glared at the backs of their crisp orange jumpsuits. The clippers hummed and hair fell in piles as the barbers prepped the new arrivals.

The warden began, "Welcome to Hell's Gate. We are a sedation incarceration facility. Thirteen years ago, researchers found they could induce hibernation in Arctic voles using a succinylcholine derivative. Today, you are the beneficiaries of that research. You shall be put into deep sleep with something we call Dante's Tea. You shall not dream. Body temperatures shall be kept near normal at eighty-eight degrees, and you shall age normally. As per federal law, an electro-stimulator program shall keep the muscular systems in working order. As per federal law, inmates shall be revived if they display conclusive life-threatening symptoms.

29

Otherwise, you shall be awakened only if you have served out your sentence, or . . ." the warden smirked, "if Hell freezes over!"

He paused and looked at the guards, who chuckled on cue.

"Wilson! I understand we have some rather infamous guests."

Ramsey nodded to a waiting female guard who tapped her wrist imprint. A hologram of the prisoner and his profile appeared.

The first barber finished and spun his chair around. Bob Braga, flexed his linebacker shoulders, glared at the warden, and tested his restraints.

Ramsey read from the profile. "Bob G. Braga, a.k.a. 'Bob the Basher,' killed three Yankee fans with a baseball bat." The warden smiled, tapped his wrist, and the hologram changed to the *New York Times* sports page. "Yankees six, Boston two," he chuckled. "How far out is Boston, Wilson?"

"Mathematically eliminated, sir," the female guard replied dispassionately.

Clang! Bob lunged at the warden and growled, "I'll see you in Hell."

Ramsey sneered and pointed to a dark stairway leading down. "Hell is through that door and down those stairs, where you're going. I only do short visits."

The second barber finished and spun the next inmate around.

This guy could have won an Alfred Hitchcock look-alike contest. The Warden tapped his wrist and examined the perp sheet. "Doctor Fleischer, or should I say 'Doktor Fleischer.' You didn't just pad your bills, you ordered extra surgeries. How many, Wilson?"

"Hard to tell, sir. Prosecutor said there were black market organs from fourteen corpses—hearts, kidneys, lungs, eyeballs."

"Parts-R-Us, huh?"

Doctor Fleischer surveyed Ramsey and pursed his lips. "Zee rare blood types are worth millions. Vat type are you, Herr Warden?"

Ramsey chortled, "I do like an entrepreneurial spirit."

He moved to the last inmate. Reverend Branson's eyes burned with inner vision and a messianic ego. The warden leaned in to look at a red cross branded on the reverend's neck.

"Tsk, tsk, tsk." He turned to Wilson. "Serial killers these days. Don't they know tattoos are permanent, that they will wear that mark the rest of their lives?" The warden touched his imprint. "And, the most infamous of all, Reverend Branson, "The Prophet." How many, Wilson?"

"Thirty-two murders, sir, if you include the slayings carried out by his cult members. Some of whom are already our guests," Wilson announced.

"Murders? Sacrifices, predestined," Branson murmured as he slowly turned his head. "I see souls, Warden. I see yours and it's wanting."

Ramsey stared at him. "Now, that's creepy. How many cult members do we have, Wilson?"

"Twelve, like the apostles."

Ramsey smirked. "It'll be like a big sleep-over."

The guards snickered.

"You dare mock me. Judgment day is coming. I shall be vindicated in Heaven," Reverend Branson retorted.

The warden paused. "Wilson, are we in Heaven?"

"No, sir."

"How do you know?"

"Because, I guard the gates of Hell, sir. I'm an atheist. They'd never let me near Heaven."

The warden leaned close. "It seems those 'sacrifices' took you in the wrong direction, Reverend." He nodded to the barbers who zapped each inmate in the back of the neck with a pneumatic syringe. "That's just somethin' to calm you down." He looked at the guards. "Let's get 'em out of here. It's bedtime."

The warden led the train of guards and shuffling prisoners toward the stairwell. Above the opened double steel doors, bracketed by two demons, a sign read: *"ABANDON ALL HOPE, YE WHO ENTER HERE."*

The warden pointed up and sneered, "Dante, my favorite."

Down the stairs, another set of double steel doors secured the second floor. An officer punched a code into a keypad, a lock clicked, and they entered a broad hallway demarcated every thirty feet by doors. The dark institutional gray tones sucked the life from the lighting, lending the hall a surreal illusion of infinite recession.

The warden stopped at room seven and opened the door. Its dark interior reared, broken only by the glow of hundreds of green and red diodes. He flipped a light switch, revealing two dozen sarcophagi stacked double high on steel racks. Three of the sarcophagi, tilted forward with tubes and coiled wires, awaited occupants. The parade of guards, technicians, and chained inmates filed inside.

The Gates of Hell

Two guards waved Bob the Basher into the first pod. He spun and head butted one, but the other guard zapped him with a taser. The officer recovered and caught Bob as he slumped to the floor. They wrestled him into the pod.

"Thanks for participating in our coffins-for-killers program," the taser-wielding guard spat.

A technician came forward, hurriedly hooked up an IV. He sneered at the limp form in the coffin. "Good night and good riddance."

Doctor Fleischer held up his hands as a gesture of cooperation and climbed into the pod. The med tech stepped forward and hooked him to the system. The doctor blinked, almost nodded off, and looked at the pod control panel. "No system ist perfect."

Reverend Branson stepped into a pod, but lifted his chin defiantly. "Isaiah 65:17, 'For, behold. I create new heavens and new earth and the former shall not be remembered nor come to mind.'" The med tech attached the IV as the reverend continued, "He shall leave only the righteous and—"

Zap! A guard hit him with the taser.

A second guard objected, "He was cooperating. Why the hell you do that?"

The aggressive guard shrugged. "I never liked Sunday School."

Chapter IV

Hope is the Thing with Feathers

Nurse Emily Bloom had worked in neonatal care, had seen heart-warming near miracles and heart-breaking pathos. Her dad once called her soft-hearted for crying at weddings and funerals, but witnessing the highs and lows of the human condition through newborn innocents had toughened her emotionally. She learned not to take it home, learned to focus on the functional, to give the past its due, but center her attention where needed—the present. These days, she worked in adult critical care. In dealing with adults, she found it easier to let those practical day-to-day functions crowd out her natural tendency to become involved emotionally.

Emily thought about what to say as she pushed the wheelchair toward Jason Adam's room. She entered with her usual perky smile. Jason Adams lay quiet, stoic, but gloom hung in the air like a shroud.

"Mr. Adams, oh, I just learned that it's Dr. Adams. You should have told me you are a psychologist. I would have brought my daughter in for some free counseling."

Jason couldn't help but smile. It felt strange. Recently, a smile stayed so far away, so inaccessible for him. "How old is she?"

"Anna is sixteen." Emily opened the locket around her neck. "This is an old picture."

"She's lovely. Teen years can be challenging. The process of individuation is awkward, but necessary. Of course, it gets better once a new steady state is established." Jason stood. "I can walk."

"Insurance rules. We put you in wheels." Emily helped Jason gather bags of personal items, rolling oxygen tank, tubes, and pills. "Is anyone at home to help?"

"I'm . . . I'm not sure."

"Your wife never made it back after you regained consciousness?"

Jason shook his head. "She probably feels guilty and wants to avoid confrontation."

Emily frowned and squeezed his shoulder. "I'm so sorry." Emily pushed him down the hall to the elevator. "Children? Relatives who can help out at home?"

"No. No children. My sister is in Ohio. I'll be alright. I can get around with these rolling O_2 bottles."

"Do you have the number for the supplier? They will deliver."

"Yeah. I'll stock up."

Emily wheeled Jason to the main doors, stopped and peered outside. "What taxi company would you like?"

"Any."

As she left to flag down a ride for him, Jason turned to look back at the sign above the hospital lobby area—words he had seen many times as a volunteer. Set out in relief from the wall, the letters seemed to float on clouds:

A Hope in Hell

"'Hope' is the thing with feathers
That perches in the soul,
And sings the tune without the words,
And never stops at all,"

—Emily Dickinson

What he had pointed out as comforting words to others who suffered grief and loss, seemed bittersweet now that he was on the receiving end.

Emily returned. "Dickinson, my favorite."

"Yeah. Very nice."

"The taxi pulled in. Goodbye, Dr. Adams. Hope is always on the shelf here at Mercy Providence. I wish you the best."

* * * * *

Before last week, the house often felt too quiet and in need of children running and playing but, now, it felt absolutely tomb-like. *Jason Adams, crypt-keeper.* Recognizing the depression didn't help, at least not in the short run. It would take time to review the events, categorize them, and fit them into a fractured world view.

The stairs, just like the 2,300-square-foot house, proved too much. Jason slept downstairs on the couch, cooked, took the pills, and called for delivery of more oxygen cylinders. He even went to the store, feeling like a geriatric rolling the oxygen bottle down the aisle.

His strength improved, and he didn't really need the supplemental oxygen for just walking around the house. He looked up cardiomyopathy on the Internet and found the prognosis the same as the doctor said—almost hopeless.

He finally reached Elaina, who confirmed she felt guilty and didn't want to be there when he returned from the hospital to cause more stress. She finally agreed to come over and talk, though.

Ding-dong.

Jason looked out the window. Elaina's Mercedes sat in the driveway. He turned off his oxygen bottle and removed the tube before opening the front door. She wore a white dress, sunglasses, and matching purse. He frowned.

Why do women dress to the nines when they end a relationship? "You don't have to knock. This is still your home."

"I did not want to surprise you. You look better."

"I feel a little stronger. Let's go to the kitchen."

Honk! A truck pulled up. "Oh. The oxygen bottles I ordered. This will only take a minute."

"Fine, I have personal things to gather."

The delivery man rolled several large gas cylinders and a crate of smaller portable bottles into the garage. Jason signed off, closed the overhead door, and felt a shortness of breath from the effort. By the time he got to the kitchen nook, Elaina was carrying out a bag of her personal things from the bedroom. Jason sat down and took some restful deep breaths.

"Looks like you've made up your mind."

Elaina set her bag down and entered the nook area, but did not sit. "I am not . . . did not come to this country for money, for citizenship. I came here for you and this life. But, you and I want different things." She leaned against the counter and played with the salt and pepper shakers. "You are so smart. You know some things of what is in everyone's head, but other things you are *doorak-nik*. I am thirty-eight years. I don't want to be mother."

Jason had planned to coax Elaina back, but heard the finality in her voice. He didn't know what to say. Everything had changed so much, any argument about family seemed moot. He pointed to his chest and opened his mouth, but no words came out.

"You and I want different things." Elaina tightened her lips and looked away from him. "Divorce is best for both of us." She turned and picked up her bag. "I'm sorry." She strode out, and closed the door without looking back.

* * * * *

NOAA, National Oceanic and Atmospheric Administration Office
Princeton, New Jersey

Dr. Bill Johnson, head of the Geophysics Fluid Dynamics Laboratory on the University of Princeton campus, grumbled and bit his lip. He was happy to have someone of Dr. Girard's stature visit, but unannounced at three o'clock on a Friday?

Does he think we have nothing better to do than drop everything and accommodate him?

Johnson specialized in atmospheric science, not in oceanography, and Dr. Wilkinson, the lead oceanographer, was away attending a conference in

Washington, D.C. What could Girard possibly want to say in person? Wouldn't an email suffice?

His secretary led Dr. Girard and a younger man into his office. He shook hands and offered them a chair.

"Welcome. This is an honor."

"Dr. Johnson, thank you for seeing us on short notification. My assistant Michael Chennault. He is sometimes my translator, also a graduate student in physical oceanography."

"I assume you're here about our work on ocean currents. Unfortunately, Dr. Wilkinson, our head of research, isn't—"

"*Oui et non*, Dr. Johnson. I am worried of possible immediate danger from the recent GRACE data showing a pressure build-up along the Pacific rift. We think of most volcanic activity as being localized, but this could upset the ocean, ahh—"

Michael took over. "We are concerned about the Pacific deep ocean sinks consisting of mostly dissolved organic carbon, methane clathrates, hydroquinone, and urea. Interactions with volcanic gases could cause a chain reaction, upsetting the ocean circulation and suddenly releasing a massive amount of gas."

Bill sat back and crossed his legs. *Is this guy for real?* "I've heard of the increase in volcanic activity along the Pacific rift, but no one has sounded alarms."

Girard leaned forward. "Recent gravity readings along the East Pacific rift, the Antarctic Ridge, and Indian Ridge, all show a buildup of mass that could lead to a global event."

"Global event?" Bill furrowed his eyebrows. "You think this might eventually affect weather, ocean currents?"

Girard and his assistant looked at each other. They both shook their heads. Girard turned back and leveled his gaze. "A Level Four Existential Event."

Bill involuntarily squirmed. *An existential event—a threat to the human species!*

"Dr. Girard, if this is an emergency, you should contact the Federal Emergency Management Agency."

"*Non, non*, and they will not listen to a voice in the . . ." He paused, clearly searching for the word.

"Wilderness," Michael supplied.

"If I could work with Dr. Wilkinson, show him the models, get the latest GRACE data. Then come to you. They might listen to you."

Why on my watch? Bill's mind reeled. Millennialists and doomsday-sayers have a long history. So far, though, they've been zero and too many to count: the UFO Heaven's Gate cult, the Branch Davidians, Jim Jones, even some of the mainstream Christians. He knew the fate of alarmists from within a bureaucracy—the unemployment line.

"I believe Wilkinson is in Washington, D. C. I'll email him and—" Bill looked up. He saw it in their eyes—nervous fear, almost panic. "I'll give him a call. Get him here as soon as possible."

* * * * *

At seven that evening, Richard Wilkinson swiped his I.D. card, heard the lock clack open, and entered the NOAA center. As instructed, he'd left in the middle of a conference, grabbed his bags, and drove three hours and ten minutes to the Princeton lab. As he drove, his anger gave way to morbid curiosity.

Why?

Dr. Johnson's words made no sense: "Dr. Jean Girard, possibly urgent, false positive, latest GRACE data, confirmed seismic activity."

If it was a true emergency, they should contact FEMA. If seismic, they should contact U.S.G.S. Why him, why an oceanographer?

Wilkinson marched straight to Johnson's office. Nobody there. He walked to the east wing and opened the door to the laboratory's data center. The scene confounded him even more. Dr. Johnson and two men bent over his computer keyboards.

What are these people doing at my workstation? And, what has gotten Iron Butt out from behind his desk? Dr. Johnson's suit coat lay in a pile, tie gone, sleeves rolled up. *Shit. This ain't good.*

Johnson glanced over, straightened up, took in a deep breath and let out a long exhale. "Dick, this is Dr. Jean Girard and his assistant, Michael . . . ahh . . ."

Girard rose and shook his hand.

"Michael Chennault." The young man spoke without turning his head.

"Dick, are you familiar with Girard's theories on deep ocean circulation?" He didn't wait for an answer. While he stood looking at a wall-mounted monitor showing the path of the GRACE satellite, Johnson dialed his cell phone. "I'm calling NASA. The satellite passed over the South Pacific about an hour ago. It won't make another pass for seventy-two hours. I'm going to see if we can get it redirected."

Wilkinson looked at Girard. "What's going on?"

"The GRACE satellite recorded a massive swelling along the southern Pacific rift. Gravitational readings were unprecedented."

Wilkinson widened his eyes. "Higher?"

"*Beaucoup plus haut*. A mass shift of over a fifty thousand gigatonnes."

"Sea level rise?"

Michael chimed in, "I'm getting the deep ocean buoy grid data now."

Johnson spoke loudly into his cell. "Chad, this is Dr. Johnson at the NOAA Fluid Dynamics Lab in Princeton."

* * * * *

Chad Robinson answered through his car audio system as he drove home from the Kennedy Space Center in Florida. "Hello, Bill. Don't you people ever go home? It's after six."

"Have your folks there alerted you to recent geologic anomalies in the South Pacific?"

"Nothing special. I think there was something about potential volcanic activity last week."

"Yeah. And, the GRACE satellite pass an hour ago showed a mass shift that's off the charts. That's what I'm calling about. We'd like a redirect for another—"

The NASA director interrupted, "Whoa, Bill. One reading doesn't mean the world's ending. It could be contact with space debris, instrument error, even a solar flare."

"Chad, we checked those possibilities. It's not one reading, it's across a quarter of the hemisphere. Dr. Jean Girard is here, and he's been following this for the past week. I mean we are talking a thousand Krakatoas."

"Do you know how many experiments you'd be mucking up. The science boys will have my head. Not to mention the fuel it'll take to—"

"Chad, I know what happens to department heads who cry wolf, but right now I'm praying I'm wrong. There will definitely be a tidal wave associated with this bulge, so if we're wrong, worst case scenario is we gain a few hours early warning for coastal communities, saving lives. If Girard is right, though, we could face an existential event."

A long silence fell on the other end of the line.

"NOAA will cover any costs associated with—"

"Jesus, Bill." Robinson pulled off the next freeway ramp. "I'm turning around. We'll either look like Chicken Littles or heroes. Shit! I'll call you as soon as we can get it done."

* * * * *

Jason Adams felt as though a proverbial rug had been pulled out from under him—still in shock, still in the denial stage, still wondering how life could go from comfortable, productive, and stable, to a train wreck in an instant. He replayed the prognosis over and over.

Your job is to wait . . . Ninety percent chance of a fatal reoccurrence within a year . . . AB negative, RH, other factors. The doctor had not given him numerical chances, just: "At your age you're not at the top of the donor recipient list."

Jason looked up the data and did the calculation, twenty-two others in front of him and, on average, only eight matching hearts a year. New younger transplant recipients could bump him even farther down the list.

Jason opened the lower cabinet of the entertainment center and pulled out several video cubes. Watching home movies would be emotionally draining, but he needed grounding, maybe something cathartic to face up to this new reality. He started at the beginning: pictures of his parents; 3D videos of him and his sister—he a toddler, his sister a rug rat; his father's funeral, school pictures in sequence, showing the progression from child to adolescent to gangly young adult; a prom, a tux, his date in a sky-blue dress.

Whatever happened to Margaret Wheeler? Jason let out a deep sigh. *Married, last I heard.*

The next cube held pictures of his college days. Mom dropping him off, his first dorm room, receiving an honors award, on-stage in bit parts, then his first and only major role—Hamlet. . . *To be or not to be.*

Jason put the cube down and spoke aloud. "Well, that wasn't as much fun as I hoped it would be. Shit!"

Tears welled in his eyes. *Where did the time go? I wanted a family! Too late now.*

After a moment, he stood.

"Well, Jason Adams, you gotta live in the present. Find whatever joy you can in the nooks and eddies of human existence."

Removing the oxygen tube, he paced back and forth. When he breathed deeply, his ribs protested with a sharp pain. *Alright, no contact sports.* "But, I think I can get down to the hospital and do some volunteer work. Yeah."

Jason called Mercy-Providence. "Hello, Janet. How's my favorite RN?" They exchanged some pleasantries and she asked the purpose for his call. "Put me down tomorrow morning for the usual rounds?" He listened. "I have, yes, but I'm feeling better." Another pause. "Thanks, I'll see you then."

* * * * *

Dr. Johnson wondered about his mental stability. On one hand, he felt like a kid again, back when curiosity was the sole driver of desire and the world stretched out in an unending supply of endorphin-generating mystery and wonder.

When did I lose that young scientific mind undistracted by the real world of people and relationships? On the other hand, the knot in his stomach clenched in pure fear, terror that he stood on a precipice witnessing the unimaginable. *A front row seat!*

Bill ran a mental schedule: hours to confirm the data, hours to convince the bureaucracy, hours to get word out to the other agencies and report it up the line. *Hopeless, the agencies will react too slowly.* Emphasize the urgency. Bring the National

Science Advisor in, get him on board, bypass the bullshit, and call the president.

Michael put up grid data on ocean currents. "Dr. Wilkinson. What do you make of this?"

Wilkinson tapped Michael's shoulder. "Let me in there." Michael yielded the station to its proprietor. Wilkinson reorganized the data onto a map of the South Pacific. "Shit. Look at this. I've never seen anything like it. There's a bulge. It's not caused by seismic activity or it would show up as a point source. He turned and stared hard at Girard.

"My theory. If the bulge along the rift is purely gaseous, it could cause this kind of event. It may—"

Bill cleared his throat and coughed. "Two minutes until the GRACE satellite crosses the prime meridian."

Girard continued, "*De Fait*, if the gases release slowly over time, it may cause disturbances in the ocean currents, a significant increase of greenhouse gases, localized extinctions, and atmospheric . . . ahh . . . weather pattern changes." He shot a glance back at Bill. "If there is a sudden release, something that massive, the gases could react with deep ocean carbon reservoirs, destabilizing clathrates and releasing enough carbon dioxide into the lower atmosphere to cause hypercapnia and hypoxia—a Nyos Effect."

Wilkinson's gaze shot from Girard to Dr. Johnson. "Bill?"

He returned a grim stare. "Most of the planet would suffocate." He shrugged his shoulders. "Maybe, we just don't know. Here it is. Coming over the Solomon Islands."

Hope is the Thing with Feathers

The four scientists fell silent as the data came in. Each stared in disbelief. Bill turned away as if avoiding a gruesome scene from a horror movie. Wilkinson broke the spell, seizing a calculator and plugging in numbers. Girard moved to a computer, doing the same.

"Shit! It can't do that. It's growing." Wilkinson held up his calculator.

Girard wiped a hand across his forehead. "*'A ce moment*, the data is feeding into my program. We'll know in about seven minutes."

Johnson's cell phone rang. He answered, "Chad. You see this?"

"For Christ sakes, Bill. What does it mean? There is only a skeleton staff here. We don't know what to make of it."

"In a few hours, we'll know if it fits Girard's theory. If it does, I'll need your help to get some warnings out, to get this up the line." The earlier excitement, he'd felt, now flat-lined, and his voice came out even and stoic. "We'll stay on it. Overnight here until we get confirmation."

Chad's dour reply came over the speakers. "Affirmative. I'll request a visual from one of our military satellites."

"Yeah. That would be good."

"Shit, Bill. I've got a family."

* * * * *

Bill called his wife and told her of a potential emergency that would require an overnight at the office. The four scientists crushed through possible scenarios, and waited as each satellite pass built a convincing picture of an unprecedented coming catastrophe. He grabbed a couple catnaps between passes, but most of the scientists waited with such dread, sleep was impossible.

At seven in the morning the NOAA computer, in the Princeton Lab, took in another round of satellite data, fed it into Jean Girard's program, and crunched possible outcomes. Dr. Girard pointed to the graph, showing the other three scientists the volume of gas and the possible impacts.

"That volume at those pressures could be over a hundred thousand gigatonnes. The gases are probably venting now. How *rapide,* how explosive, is the question."

Wilkinson looked back at his own computer monitor. "The Deep Ocean buoys show another increase in sea level. Sixteen feet above normal!"

"It's time to sound the alarms. I'll start with Ewa Beach." Bill called the National Tsunami Warning Center in Hawaii and reached a staff seismologist. "Are you picking up the DART buoy data in the Southern Pacific?"

"Yes, sir. Very strange, but there's been no unusual seismic activity."

"Yes, there has. Nothing that would be considered an earthquake, but there's a huge shift in mass along the Pacific Rift. We think there will be only a small tsunami, but a hell of a storm associated with it."

"Sir, I have strict criteria in putting out a tsunami warning."

"Look. If this thing has the gas volumes and pressures the gravity readings indicate, it'll be catastrophic. Call your director, connect me with—"

"Bill, we're getting the military satellite pictures. Lots of cloud cover."

Ring. Ring. Wilkinson answered the phone on his desk and passed it across. "Bill, it's Chad."

"Hold on, young man." Johnson switched phones. "Chad?"

"Bill. There were clear skies throughout the South Pacific, now a storm the size of Australia has formed in the last few hours. Our pressure bubble is making its own weather system."

The large wall monitor showed the storm formation from the vantage point of outer space. Dark cloud cover appeared along the line of the Pacific rift. Dr. Johnson put the NASA director on speakerphone as the four scientists watched.

Girard pointed to the western edge of the storm. "It's spreading!"

They could hear Chad in the background over the speaker. "Get a fix on that point, right there . . . Okay . . . What? You sure?" . . . "Bill. That thing is expanding at a hundred and fifty miles per hour. Is that possible?"

Girard chimed in, "It is consistent with my theory. I believe the release of volcanic gases is disturbing the deep ocean sink, upsetting the balance, and bringing up an even greater mass of gases. *Merde!*"

"How far will it spread?" Chad's voice turned solemn.

There was a profound silence as the three scientists stared at Girard. He opened his mouth, but nothing came out. Girard turned away from them. "As long as it is over the ocean it will continue to increase. When it hits the mainland, the storm front will be powerful enough to cover the continent, even the world."

"I've got the Tsunami Warning Center on the line. Chad, can we send them the satellite data?"

"I'll get a tech on it," Chad replied.

Johnson turned back to the warning center. "Young man, you can send out storm warnings?"

"Yes. And, I can do small boat advisories," the seismologist confirmed.

"I advise you to do so immediately and get your director out of bed. Tell him . . . tell him it's a major event. You have my number. Have him call me ASAP." Bill hung up. "When is the next satellite pass?"

Michael checked the time. "Eighty-eight minutes."

Dr. Johnson paused, walked into the next room, and phoned his wife again. "Hi, Honey . . . Good, that'll be fine. Listen, Honey, we have a storm coming our way. I would like you to pick up the kids, bring them home, and stay put. Very important, keep everybody in one place for the next twenty-four hours . . . Yes, call your sister. I'll update you as soon as I can . . . I love you."

Johnson returned to the war room as Girard pointed to the screen showing the military satellite view of the storm. "It has reached the Cook Islands by now. Dr. Johnson?"

"I'm on it. I'm calling the international airport in Rarotonga. I don't know who else to call."

Michael looked up numbers. "It's administered by New Zealand. I have some government offices listed."

Girard turned to Wilkinson. "If there is a Nyos Effect, there will be no one to answer."

Wilkinson shook his head. "Surely some people will survive. Indoors? Young people?"

Michael cut in. "The gases within the storm may have such high CO_2 content it induces hypercapnia—too much carbon dioxide in the blood causing disorientation within the first minute, then loss of consciousness and death within two to five."

"My God. A level-four extinction event." Wilkinson looked back at Bill as if looking for leadership, a mediator, a guide to indicate how to react to the unthinkable.

"Hello, hello!" Bill glanced at his colleagues. "I got somebody at Rarotonga." He put his cell on speakerphone. "Hello, is this Rarotonga Airport?"

"I'm sorry, sir. This is Auckland International," an airline employee answered. "Your call was forwarded. A storm has cut communications with Rarotonga. Flights in and out of the Cook Islands are canceled for now."

"Do you know of any other forms of communication with the islands? Is there underwater cable or shortwave radio?"

"I wouldn't know, sir."

"Do you know any government offices that might have communication with anyone in Rarotonga?

"I do not. I'm sorry. I have other calls coming in." *Click.*

A Hope in Hell

Bill looked up at the military satellite view. "American Samoa. There'll be government offices."

"And, I'll try Tonga." Michael pulled out his cell phone.

Bill solemnly listened to the ring tones as calls to American Samoa and Tonga went unanswered. He tried a second number. He jumped up to his feet when he got an answer. "Hello, hello, this is Dr.—"

"If you have reached these offices after hours, please leave a message and someone will get back to you."

"Damn, the system's working but nobody is . . ." Bill looked at his colleagues. "We still need to confirm a Nyos Effect. I will call FEMA, see what they have so far."

He eventually reached the head of FEMA. "Dr. Nadeen, this is Dr. Johnson. I'm head of research at the NOAA lab in Princeton. We have serious concerns about the storm in the South Pacif—"

Yamin Nadeen interrupted, "Yes. It has come to our attention, appearing out of nowhere. It's so new we haven't even named it yet."

"We have not been able to communicate with anyone within the storm area. We think that gas levels inside the storm front may be anoxic. If so—"

"Dr. Johnson, loss of communication with remote islands of Micronesia during typhoons and during monsoon season is typical. Cell towers, satellite receivers, even short wave might be out. I wouldn't worry too much until the storm passes and they have twenty-four hours to restore communications."

"This is not a typical storm! It's too broad and powerful. We think it is driven by a volcanic release of gases and those gases may cause hypercapnia and hypoxia within the storm area."

"What you are saying is completely unprecedented. What is the basis for this? I would need hard evidence. I do not even have a warning protocol for such a thing. We have sent out storm surge warnings to Hawaii and the West Coast— South America, Mexico, and as far as north as Los Angeles and—"

"Look, if it is anoxic, this could be a level-four existential event! We have to warn people!" Bill rubbed his forehead in exasperation.

There was a moment of silence before Nadeen spoke. "What would you have me do, send out a warning that the world is ending? What actions do we tell people to take?" Silence. "I need incontrovertible proof."

Dr. Johnson's stomach tightened another notch. He knew this would happen, the system would react too slowly, that billions of people were doomed. *His family! He had to get home. Try and save them.* He needed to demonstrate this not just with science but with theater, something dramatic. "Dr. Nadeen, stay available. We'll send you a satellite feed as soon as we can set it up. Also, may I suggest a name? . . . Cassandra."

Johnson ended the call and redialed Ewa Beach, Hawaii. The same young staffer answered. Neither his boss nor any of the senior scientists had responded.

"I didn't get your name, young man."

"Joel. Joel Becker."

"Joel, I want you to work with me to set up a video feed over the military emergency communications system. I'll get FEMA to authorize it."

"Yes, sir."

"Okay, hold on." Bill called FEMA back and arranged for Ewa Beach to tie into the military system.

Michael broke in. "The GRACE satellite is passing over Micronesia."

Wilkinson looked on. "Oh, shit! Boss, better look at this."

The four scientists stared at the screen with their mouths open. Bill felt the acid in his chest. *Focus, focus.*

Girard was the first to voice his assessment. "The pressure has increased throughout the southern hemisphere and is spreading northward along the Pacific Mid-Ocean Ridge." Pointing to the satellite feed on the wall screen. "I'm afraid new storm fronts are forming. *C'est tres mauvais.* This is very bad."

Bill covered his cell phone. "When will it reach Hawaii?"

Michael did a quick calculation. "The leading front, in one and one-half hours."

Bill stepped away and returned the cell phone to his ear. "Joel, how's it going?

"I have the video cam set up and I called the number you gave me."

"Okay, I'm patching in." He brought a video feed on his computer showing a nervous young man staring into the camera. "Hi, Joel, this feed was built to survive a nuclear blast, so it should hold up during the storm. Do you have a carbon dioxide meter there?"

Hope is the Thing with Feathers

"There's CO_2 and O_2 meters in the storage room."
"Get both, please. Set them up so we can see the readouts."

* * * * *

Jason couldn't handle any more reality. He spent the evening with his favorite pie, ice cream, and comedy classics—old classics they seldom made anymore: mindless, universal physical comedy from Mel Brooks, Jim Carrey, Leslie Nielsen. The movies featured prideful, quirky characters whose own flaws bumped incongruously against reality. They took his mind off his situation, a welcomed temporary relief.

After several hours of zoning out, he still couldn't sleep. Flipping channels, he caught a local broadcast.

"Tropical storm Cassandra is moving toward the south west coast of the United States. The National Weather Service has issued storm warnings as far north as San Francisco."

Jason turned it off. No reality! *"Nothing of kings, nothing of crowns, bring on the lovers, lions, and clowns."* He queued up another comedy. At two in the morning, he finally drifted off to sleep.

* * * * *

Within an hour winds began gusting against the windows of NOAA's Ewa Beach Research Center. In Princeton, Dr. Johnson watched and occasionally asked Joel a perfunctory question or two.

Otherwise, Joel sat in silence. National news channels covered the storm hitting the Hawaiian Islands, but strangely without the usual videos of waves hammering the beaches or intrepid surfers braving the storm surf. Within another half-hour, the Hawaiian sky darkened to twilight and high winds struck the windows next to Joel. The electricity cut out, dimming the room further, but battery backup kept the computer running and emergency lighting revealed the fear in Joel Becker's face.

Bam! The young staffer jumped as debris struck the window. "Holy cow! This is worse than I thought. Maybe I should have gone to a storm shelter."

Bill's face flushed with guilt. "I . . . I'm . . . Oh, God. What have I—"

Girard broke in. "Young man, *a pas du tout*. I don't think that would help."

Joel's breathing became labored. Girard pointed to the gas meters. "Carbon dioxide is moving steadily upward from 0.1 part per million, one part per million, two . . . three . . . five . . . parts per million. Normal oxygen levels are dropping . . . twenty-one parts per million to eighteen ppm."

"Crap, what's going on?" Joel turned to the meters. "Shit! Why is the oxygen dropping? The carbon dioxide? What the hell?" The CO_2 increased to eight parts per million. Joel labored for breath and looked directly into the camera, his lips red. "You knew this. You—"

Wham! A window broke, sending glass shards over Joel, who ducked and curled up under his desk. Thick debris obscured the meter readouts.

Hope is the Thing with Feathers

The four scientists looked on in horror. Only a melee of shapes and shadows played on the video and howling wind filled the audio. Suddenly Joel's face appeared. Gasping, he held the L.E.D. display up close to the camera—the readout, 10 ppm CO_2.

Bill flinched. *Too high for humans to survive.*

Joel sank to the floor. His shadowy form shuddered and stilled.

Chapter V

The End of the Holocene

Jason awoke early and did his morning routine. Occasionally, he paused and took some deep breaths, but didn't use the oxygen. His ribs felt a little better—*I can do the rounds at the hospital without dragging the O₂ bottle around.* However, when he exited the house and opened the garage door, the stiff breeze, heavy with moisture, made breathing a bit more taxing than indoors. So, he threw a small portable oxygen bottle in the front seat and rolled a larger cylinder into the trunk, just in case.

Jason drove through unusually light freeway traffic. Though accustomed to Seattle weather, the cool mugginess and dim light from the heavy cloud cover lent an ominous gloom to the morning. As he pulled into the parking lot, he thought about entering through the front lobby, walking down to the critical care wing and saying hi to the kindly nurse who had taken care of him.

Emily. Yeah, like the poet.

He reminded himself of his condition and decided to limit today's activities to his usual haunt for volunteering over the past several years—the recovery wing. Jason parked in the back, exited, and walked to a rear entrance. He rolled his oxygen bottle along behind him, but planned to leave it at the nurse's station. A couple of maintenance men placed sheets of plywood over some windows.

The End of the Holocene

Must be doing some major maintenance.

Jason sensed something unusual with the staff. Nearly a dozen hospital personnel gathered around a monitor at the critical care nurse station. The head nurse, Ms. Janet Bradley, saw him. A couple of the R.N.s and the custodian said hello and asked how he was doing.

Ms. Bradley stepped aside, "Dr. Adams, I didn't expect you to come, with all the storm warnings and such."

"I didn't listen to the radio. What's going on?"

"Hundred-fifty mile-per-hour winds, movin' up the coast."

"My gosh. That's a hurricane. We never get hurricanes up here."

"A very serious hurricane." Ms. Bradley nodded to her extra staff. "The hospital is on civil alert code orange. All ambulances are on deck and expecting casualties."

The television blared over the conversation. "Cassandra, a category-five storm, is unprecedented in its size and intensity. It has already hit the southwest coast of California, wiping out communications. We lost contact with our affiliates in San Diego and . . ."

Jason's eyebrows furrowed. "Damn. Maybe I better head home."

Beep. Beep. Beep.

"We interrupt this program for an emergency message from the Federal Emergency Broadcast System. This is not a test."

The nurse's forehead furrowed. "I don't know, Mr. Adams. You may be better off here. This hospital is built for hell and high water."

Jason stretched over several staffers to peek at the television monitor.

". . .citizens . . . *hiss* . . . to shelter in place . . . *hiss* . . . food . . .supplies . . . *hiss.*"

"I think you're right. Well, I might as well do something productive. What do you have this morning?"

The head nurse reached for a tablet and tapped a couple commands. "These three, all new. Ms. Olafson, middle-aged, female, miscarriage. Physically she'll be fine, but she is very upset."

"Husband?"

"In the military, deployed, and won't be back for a couple months." She passed the tablet to Jason. "It's all here. I better get busy myself and make sure the hatches are battened down."

Jason nodded.

* * * * *

Bill sat a moment as tears coursed down his cheeks. *Focus, focus.* Taking a couple of deep breaths, he dialed FEMA.

"Dr. Nadeen, you saw it?" His speech came out monotone, almost robotic. He paused for the reaction. "Yes, I can confirm that. The final readout we saw was ten percent CO_2. I am confirming this is a Level Four Existential Event. Dr. Nadeen, time is short, you must call the president."

The End of the Holocene

"My direct access is really indirect. I must go through the chief of staff." The lack of urgency in Dr. Nadeen's voice gave Bill a sinking feeling.

The FEMA director cleared his throat. "Stay on the line. I'll need the full weight of your expertise."

* * * * *

The president's chief of staff, Gerald Sullivan, was not liked by his employees. Puritanically judgmental, he was not liked by other cabinet members, Congress, foreign heads of state, nor the media. He was curt to the point of rudeness. Gerald Sullivan did not separate work and family life well; consequently, his family didn't like him either. John Calvin would have been proud. A prominent newspaper columnist once joked that Sullivan's own mother's affection was in doubt. The writer said when Gerald came out of the womb he didn't cry, he criticized, "You call that pushing? You didn't do enough Kegel exercises, did you?"

Gerald Sullivan saw himself as the guardian of the president, thus the gatekeeper who separated the cry-wolfs from fang-and-claw political reality. So, when his phone rang after work hours and the callers told him the world was ending, he responded with skepticism.

"Dr. Nadeen, I realize this storm is a major disaster, but things like you are describing are unprecedented. I understand Hawaii has lost communications but, if it's as bad as you say, I would have heard of this through military channels."

A Hope in Hell

"The high pressure along the Pacific rift has been reported. But, the military leaders are not scientists. They don't have the latest theories on ocean carbon sinks and—" Nadeen audibly exhaled and paused.

Sullivan asked, "Dr. Johnson. I suspect this is just an unusual, major storm that knocked out communications."

"You're right, sir, when you say this is unprecedented. Nothing like this has occurred in at least six hundred million years. We have a video from Hawaii inside the storm front. It confirms Dr. Jean Girard's predictions."

The chief of staff remained skeptical. "I need to see it. But, even if this front started with high carbon dioxide levels in the South Pacific. It would surely disperse before it hit Hawaii."

Nadeen said, "Dr. Johnson is the atmospheric scientist."

"The GRACE data shows it building, not dissipating. Dr. Girard thinks the volcanic events have set off a chain reaction in the deep ocean, releasing carbon dioxide, sulfur, and methane clathrates. There may be enough mass to cover the entire surface of the earth, enough for a mass extinction. We think this meets the criteria for a Level Four Existential Event."

Sullivan paused. "Alright, show me this video."

While Sullivan viewed their video, Bill turned to the other scientists who waited for the GRACE satellite to cross over the Pacific.

The End of the Holocene

Wilkinson looked at his watch. "It's over the Atlantic right now. It'll be fifteen minutes before we get another reading along the Pacific Coast."

Girard turned to another screen showing a satellite view of a storm over the North Atlantic. "*C'est un problème!*" The maelstrom centered over Iceland with new fronts forming southward along the Mid-Atlantic Ridge.

Bill frowned at the incoming GRACE data from the North Atlantic. He didn't think his stress level could get any higher, but when he saw a bulge in the Mid-Atlantic Ridge, his adrenal and endocrine systems gave his corticoid count another jolt.

The four scientists stood in silence. Again, Girard verbalized their fears. "If that is anoxic and moves the same speed as the Cassandra storm, it will reach us in about four or five hours."

Bill turned his attention back to the phone conversation with Dr. Nadeen and the chief of staff.

" . . . understand what the meters mean. Who made this video?" Sullivan sounded incredulous.

Bill cut in, "Chief of Staff Sullivan, I made the video twenty minutes ago."

"I have to verify this with the Pentagon and get back to you," Sullivan said dismissively.

Bill Johnson's heart sank.

The other three scientists paused from their monitors to listen in on Bill's conversation.

Sullivan sounded as though he were placating a teenager. "Dr. Nadeen, you have the authority to send out category-five storm warnings, but hold off on any announcement about the carbon dioxide levels or end-of-the-world talk. We don't want to start a panic until I can confirm and get back with you."

Bill burst in, "We have to get warnings out. Goddamn it! This will hit the West Coast in a matter of hours."

"I will get back with you as soon as I can." The chief of staff hung up.

Wilkinson moaned under his breath. "What the hell good will storm warnings do?"

Bill shrugged. "We could save a few people. Tell them to find air supplies, get oxygen concentrators." He returned to the phone and the head of FEMA. "Dr. Nadeen, we have families. I'll be in cell phone contact, but we have to take steps now.

He hung up. *I knew the agencies would react too slowly.* "Shit!" *I can say I-told-you-so, but billions will die . . . schadenfreude.* He turned to the other scientists. "I thought we'd have more time." His eyes drifted toward the satellite screen. "Dr. Girard, if this is what we think, how long will it last?"

Girard shook his head. "Months, years? I do not know."

Wilkinson's voice went up an octave, "Holy shit, guys. The South Atlantic was clear ninety minutes ago. It's not now! We gotta get out of here!" Wilkinson's voice cracked, his chest heaved. "What's it going to take to survive?"

He buried his face in his hands and wept.

Bill gripped Wilkinson's shoulder. "For the short term, we need supplemental oxygen, and CO_2 scrubbers. Self-contained breathing gear will work, too, but there should be no toxicity, so full SCUBA isn't necessary. In the long term, we want oxygen generators, which need electricity. Most diesel and gasoline engines will run rough with the lower O_2 content, but they'll run. Eventually, we will have to lean out the mixture."

Michael pulled out his phone. "We can get oxygen at a medical supply store or welding shop." He searched for the nearest store.

"I have basic survival gear at the house—food, water. We need as much gasoline as we can load up. Let's take two cars, one to get the O_2, the other to get gasoline and a portable generator."

Bill slapped Wilkinson on the back. The oceanographer nodded and straightened up.

Bill stepped around and looked Wilkinson in the eye. "We can do this, Rich."

"Yeah. I can do it." His jaw clinched.

Bill gave orders. "Go with Girard. Michael, come with me. I have some calls to make."

* * * * *

Jason finished his volunteer rounds at the hospital: three new patients dealing with loss and grief. He offered comfort, assured them support from a caring community, and helped them start the process of coming to terms, the process of adjustment. Returning to the critical care station, he retrieved his bottle of oxygen. He made it through the last two hours without the supplemental oxygen, but now he rolled it into the break room and sat a while with the gas turned up. Almost compulsively, he felt in his pocket for the reassuring nitro pills, hoping to heck he would never need them.

A Hope in Hell

Another attack could be fatal . . . worse, a stroke . . . debilitating, functionally, mentally. Jason shook off his grim reverie and decided to visit the neonatal unit. He needed an affirmation of life. Then he would visit that nurse in the cardiac wing. It'd be worth the walk, show her he was doing fine, worth it for her smile. Jason exited to the hall and walked over to the nurse's station to listen in on the emergency broadcast.

". . . stay home, take cover, go to public shelters only if you can safely get there before the storm front hits. But, do not attempt to drive inland and flee. The storm is moving incredibly fast."

Jason paused, considered the long walk across the hospital, and decided to take his oxygen bottle along. Retrieving it, he paced himself, rolling the cart behind him down the wing, through the node, up a ramp, to the lobby. Once again, he paused for Emily Dickinson's poem, "Hope," displayed above the main admittance counter:

"'Hope' is the thing with feathers
That perches in the soul,

He muttered the words under his breath. This time it seemed more assuring, more meaningful. Glancing toward the front entrance, maintenance personnel placed barriers and roped off areas near the large windows. Outside, the sky darkened more, but only a fitful breeze lifted the flag. *The calm before the storm?* He turned toward Neonatal.

New life occupied half the basinets. Several babies lay in incubators with monitors. Jason stood on his toes to peer down into one incubator. The baby breathed through a ventilator and wasn't much larger than his hand. *Individual life so fragile, but species survival so resilient.* He looked down at his own oxygen bottle and back at the ventilated baby. *I hope he makes it.* Jason resumed his walk.

As he passed the waiting area next to the Emergency entrance, he paused. People occupied all the chairs, some sat on the floor, entire families camped in the corners. An ambulance pulled up outside the west-facing entrance just as a hard gust hit, smacking against the glass sliding doors. *Damn, it's coming fast.* Paramedics unloaded a gurney carrying an elderly man. As the automatic doors opened, another gust sprayed dust and debris inside. A collective wail and groan issued from the people sitting near the entrance.

Jason proceeded up a ramp to the second-level nurses' station. Only one nurse worked the desk, but a teenage girl also sat behind the counter. The teen, her head buried in a book, looked tall and lanky, and wore a tight black skirt and top, nose stud, and several ear piercings. She looked like Emily. *Daughter? Naw, probably not.*

Jason nodded to the nurse. "I'm looking for Emily Bloom."

She glanced up. "She's down E-wing. Can I help you?"

"No, that's alright. I was a patient here and just dropped by to say hi. If everyone's busy, I'll come back later."

"We're putting all the post-op patients on oxygen 'cause of the storm and all. They had some maintenance malfunction. As soon as she and Mark get the oxygen system fixed, she'll be back. In fact, I'll run down and check." The nurse turned to her computer screen and the online video.

". . . hurricane force winds have struck the outer islands northwest of Washington along the Olympic Peninsula and will soon reach Seattle and the mainland."

The nurse stood up and moved around the desk. "Sounds like we are in for one heck of a blow. I'll be back in a minute." She scurried off down a hall.

Jason turned to the windows. Now, fitful gusts slammed the glass with increasing frequency. The sky darkened to twilight.

Behind him a voice caught his attention. "If you're trying to get in her pants, she's already got a boyfriend."

When he turned to the reading girl, she never looked up from her book.

"Hi, my name's Jason. Are you Emily's daughter?" No response. "Anna, isn't it?"

The girl huffed. "Did she show you that little good-girl school picture she keeps in her locket?"

"Hmm, I guess she did."

"It's *over* a year old." The girl emphasized "over" as if it were forever.

"I see you're more grown up now."

The girl gave a glib, "Whatever," and continued reading.

Wham! Another gust physically bowed the windowpanes. Jason stepped away from the glass. "We better move up the hall, away from these windows."

"I'm fine," she said dismissively.

The End of the Holocene

Jason rolled up the corridor passing the nurse's station. *Bam!* A tree branch smacked a nearby pane, startling the teenager. He walked back, stretched out a hand.

"I can bring your chair."

The teenager's face paled, anxious. No snarky riposte, she stood and gathered her books and purse. Jason picked up the chair and winced as his ribs shot a pain throughout his chest. They hurried farther into the east wing, turning right at the intersection of crossing hallways.

The desk nurse stood in front of an open room. The hospital smells lingered here—floor cleaner and antiseptics covering the smell of body fluids, aging, and death. He heard Emily's voice from within the room.

The desk nurse saw Jason and pointed. "Here she is."

Jason parked his oxygen bottle and put the chair down. "It's getting nasty out there."

The nurse grimaced. "But, duty calls." She turned and headed back down the hall.

Emily and a man with long hair and blue overalls worked on the oxygen delivery system.

She turned and paused. "Well, hello, what brings you here?" Noticing her daughter, she leaned outside the room. "Are you alright, hon?"

Jason pointed up, indicting the storm. "We thought we'd better get away from the windows."

Wham! The whole building let out a groan and swayed.

Emily nodded. "Wow! That's a good idea. Ahh . . . Dr. Adams. Good to see you're getting around."

"Yeah. I'm doing better."

Wham! Another gust hit. The lights went out. *Bang!* Windows shattered. *Whoosh.* Shards and debris whizzed down the hall.

Anna screamed. Jason closed his eyes, ducked, and covered his face and head against a thousand fragments of glass, dirt, and sand. He labored for air. Something was wrong. The air smelled like low tide. The doctor's words flashed in his head, *"Ninety percent chance of a fatal reoccurrence."* He touched his pocket, feeling for the nitro pills. *No! The French scientist? Carbon-gun, Nyos Effect. Oxygen!*

Jason sat up, eyes closed, and felt for his bottle.

He peeked between his fingers. In the dim glow of emergency lighting, Anna lay gasping for air. Half peeping, half feeling, he found the bottle valve, cranked it open, and managed the respirator's strap around his head. A few breaths . . . better . . . but he needed more. His lungs, so heavy, head light. Jason fumbled with the regulator valve and turned it, increasing the oxygen flow.

Jason took several deep breaths. As his body recovered, thoughts flooded his mind in quick succession: *I feel better, so there must be a lack of oxygen in the air. Only one oxygen supply.*

With one eye, Jason peeked at the scene in the hallway. Both Anna and Emily lay prostrate, flailing their arms. He hesitated. *What are the ethics of this?* Save the girl? But, to what good, if the rest of them died? Save Emily? Could he save them all? Instead of taking action, he vacillated as critical seconds ticked by. A strong gust peppered his skin, and he covered his face with his hands again.

Something brushed against him. He squinted with one eye, Emily. She ripped the mask from his head and placed it over her mouth. Jason gasped, filling his lungs with the unsatisfying maelstrom. With hands shielding his face, he peered at Emily and reached for the mask, but she pulled away and placed it on her daughter. Anna shuddered, but her chest expanded taking in the precious oxygen.

Jason's lungs burned. He almost reached for the respirator several times. His consciousness ebbed. Resigned to die, he closed his eyes.

A tap on his shoulder.

Jason felt the mask over his nose and mouth. Inhaling, he peered through the storm. Emily held the respirator in one hand and, with the other, she held up three fingers. He took three quick breaths. Emily pulled the mask away and placed it over her own face. *Why hadn't he done that?* Guilt welled up in his chest. *Was he a coward?*

The wind continued howling through the hallway, but the shards hitting Jason's skin lessened. Emily gave the mask to Anna and pulled her toward the hospital room. He followed with a growing ache in his chest. Just as he nodded toward blackness again, the mask came around. He took three deep inhales and passed it to Emily. They continued crawling and buddy breathing until they pushed into the nearby room, escaping the worst of the g-force winds.

The room held even less light. Jason knew each room supplied an oxygen outlet somewhere, but where? They couldn't continue three-way buddy breathing for long—too exhausting. He scanned the wall for a valve outlet, to no avail. Emily took her turn with the oxygen and then stood and stumbled to the wall. She found the second of the room's two oxygen supplies. One set of tubing ran over to the only patient in the room. Jason watched as she deftly worked. She turned both valves full on, and pulled the second coil of tubing free of the wall. Emily took several breaths, and passed it to Anna.

Jason sat with his respirator to himself when something moved. A person. The body beside him shuddered. Looking down, Jason made out the blue coveralls of the man he had seen inside the room. *The maintenance guy, Mark.*

Though not a medical doctor, Jason recognized the symptoms of hypoxia, and knew the person in front of him lay dying. He took a deep breath, pulled the mask off, and placed it over the man's face. Jason waited but . . . nothing, no response. Jason returned the respirator to his own mouth.

Emily slid over and tried to help. She straightened the man's neck and airways and motioned to Jason. He again took a deep breath and placed the respirator on the comatose maintenance man. Still no response.

His lips are red. High carbon dioxide in the blood. Jason couldn't help but think about sharing the limited oxygen supplies with another person. He thought of giving up when Emily stepped in front of him. She knelt astride the maintenance man and began chest compressions. One, two, three, four . . .

ten. Mark's chest shuddered. *Cough.* The man in blue coveralls opened his eyes.

Emily slid off him and returned to Anna, and again shared oxygen with her daughter. Jason reached toward his own respirator, but hesitated, thinking the man almost died a few seconds ago. His head hurt and that, now familiar, ache in his chest returned when Emily shouted, "Mrs. Larson!" and pointed to the room's only patient.

He rose and stumbled over to the bed and the unconscious older woman. Dizzy, his headache could have been measured on the Richter scale. He pulled her respirator off and sucked in the life-sustaining ambrosia. *My God, what if I kill her?*

Within a few breaths, his head cleared. Jason returned the mask to the patient. He tried to count three or four breaths and took the respirator. One, exhale, two, exhale, three, exhale, four. He replaced the respirator back over the patient.

The maintenance man regained his wits, sat up, and holding the respirator to his face, looked around in wild-eyed shock.

Jason took his turn at the oxygen and lurched to the door. He tried to swing it closed, but air pressure forced him to put his shoulder to it before it clicked shut. He stumbled back to the bed and the precious oxygen.

Bang! Wham! Something hit the roof. Something big. Girders groaned and the ceiling buckled inward, though it remained intact. For now, their room, their little piece of sanctuary, held. Three oxygen supplies for five people. Everyone seemed stable with Emily and Anna buddy breathing the hospital supply, Mark using Jason's portable bottle, and he and the patient sharing the other hospital outlet.

Mark waved for everybody's attention. He shouted something about mountain climbers, held up two fingers, and demonstrated how to take two short intakes with two exhales. He then pulled out a flashlight and shined it at the gauge on their only portable oxygen bottle. Jason's heart sank. The needle almost pointed to empty.

Creech. Errrk. The indented roof groaned. Mark pointed east and shouted, "There's a supply closet down the hall. Or, try and get to the basement. Oxygen generators there." Mark tapped his chest and shouted, "I'll go down the hall." He started toward the door with the portable respirator.

Jason nodded and continued buddy breathing with the unconscious woman. He again felt useless. *He had a heart condition. He couldn't . . .*

Crack! Jason looked up and watched a three-foot rip appear in the roof. *Bang! Whoosh.* The door bowed inward. Wind whistled around the edges. The door tore from its hinges, striking Mark and knocking him to the floor. Mrs. Larson's bed flipped over, tossing her against the wall. Wind whipped through the room with mythical force. Jason's heart pounded at the thought of three-way buddy breathing. He paused, thinking of Emily and her altruistic actions.

Something clicked in Jason's mind. *I'm a dead man anyway! Death—the undiscovered country.* He closed his eyes, calmed himself. The lower brain bypassed the cerebrum, and everything became clear. Jason crawled to Mark. The maintenance man lay stunned, but still conscious. Jason found the respirator from the portable bottle and placed it over Mark's face. He lunged over to Mrs. Larson and slipped the respirator over the woman's nose and mouth. Wind noise made talking impossible. He took another turn with the respirator. He moved over to tap Mark on the shoulder and pointed toward the hall. He stood, marched to the doorway, and pushed out into the din.

Chapter VI

Hail Mary

Bill Johnson called his wife and confirmed everyone had gathered at his house including her sister and family. He told her to tell others and warn them of the storm, try and convince them of the coming apocalypse, but he doubted she would succeed with many. He kept hoping for a call from the chief of staff, but nothing so far.

He and Michael Chennault took one of the government's SUVs, and drove in the evening gloom to a closed medical supply store. "There's usually a number on the window. I could call the owner. Ask him to open up for an emergency?" Bill asked, thinking out loud.

Mike shook his head. "Time. It would take too long."

"If we break in and the police come?" Bill took a deep breath. "We get arrested, we could fail. It would be too late to save my family." He turned at the end of the block and made another right into an alleyway. They stopped at a loading dock with a personnel entry and an overhead garage door at the rear of the store. "I didn't even think to bring tools. There should be a tire iron in the back."

Michael opened the back of the SUV and rummaged around. "Hey, a tool box."

"Bless those forgetful technicians. They're supposed to put that stuff away."

Michael opened the box and took out a twelve-inch monkey wrench. Bill found a hammer and a crow bar. Looking up and down the alley they crept to the back door.

Michael tried the door knob—locked. "How long do we have until the police respond?"

"I was a nerd. Never done this before. Guessing, at least five minutes. No, it would take longer for the security company to call the police, maybe ten minutes? Do it!"

Michael put the monkey wrench on the door knob and twisted. Nothing. He put his full weight on it and it slipped off. "Shit!"

"Wait a minute. There's a dead bolt, too. We're idiots." Bill tried to pry the bottom and side of the overhead garage door. It didn't budge. "Stay here, I'll go around front." Bill jogged out the alley and back to the street. A car drove by, so he waited for the headlights to pass. He took off his sport coat, wrapped his arm, and *crash* . . . punched the hammer through the front window. An alarm sounded. Pushing more of the glass plate out of the way, he climbed through, stumbled from the front room to a hallway and let Michael in the back door. Bill looked at his watch and noted the time. "We've gotta hurry."

Bill opened a double set of doors that led to the loading dock and hit the light. *Thank God.*

"Voilá. Ahh. Jackpot?"

"Yes, jackpot, my friend." Large green 2,000-psi gas bottles lined the back wall of a loading bay. Several smaller bottles stood on rolling dollies, and others were stacked in crates. "Grab this."

He and Michael quickly, but carefully, lifted a crate, made their way to the alley, and slid it into the back of the SUV.

Bill pointed. "Get the large bottles and I'll get dollies, masks, and tubing. This is all good, but we really need an oxygen generator. I'll see."

Michael wrestled eight of the ninety-pound green bottles into the vehicle. Bill ran out with a box of supplies. "There's a small oxygen generator!" He looked at the time. "Shit. It's been six minutes." He looked up the alleyway and back to Michael. "It's big. Probably three hundred pounds."

Michael calculated. "Ahh . . . a hundred-thirty-six kilograms. We can get it in."

The two men hurried inside and soon emerged with a machine the size of a dresser. They walked it back and forth, tipped it onto the bed of the SUV, and shoved it in atop the oxygen bottles.

Bill looked at Michael and smiled. "We did—"

Whirrr, wheerrrr! Red and blue lights flashed as a police cruiser sped up the alleyway toward them.

* * * * *

Warden Jeff Ramsey helped design the prison. It was his baby. Designed for one-hundred-fifty mile-per-hour winds, hundred-year floods, and nine-point-zero earthquakes—he thought it could withstand anything. When he walked into the break room, five guards looked up. Several ate popcorn, and one read the newspaper, though it was well past the union-mandated break period.

Hail Mary

Ramsey hated slack time more than General Patton hated sloppy soldiers. *This prison is so damned automated it breeds complacency.* "Where's the on-duty engineer?"

"John had to go home. Emergency, storm and all."

Ramsey's lips tightened. He stepped over to the status board and saw John had checked out an hour ago. The warden bit down on his anger and kept his voice even, "All leave should go through me."

One of the guards retorted, "He's got a wife and kids in town. A storm like this is an emergency."

"Yeah. I've always said if there is ever a nuclear war, this is where you want to be. Safer here than at home." Ramsey touched some icons on the status board. "Let's hope nothing goes wrong." He called up a view of the front gate and watched the winds whip the trees to and fro.

"Anything new on the storm?" One of the guards broke the silence.

"Pretty ominous. Wind starting up." Ramsey continued studying the monitor.

"Unusual to have a Chinook wind so far north this time of year." The guard added, "The town is going to get hit pretty hard."

"When is the last time the standby generators were tested under full load?" Ramsey asked.

"Last Friday." The guards understood Ramsey already knew that.

"Both of them?"

"They alternate, one each week." He knew that, too.

Ramsey nodded. "Fuel tanks topped off?"

"Yes, sir."

"Good, good. We're ready."

Whoomph! A gust of wind hit the building. The lights flickered. The concrete structure groaned even though it was anchored deep into the bedrock. The room dimmed to only the emergency lighting. *Vrrroooom.* Ramsey felt the vibration as the generator started and the lights came back on.

"I'll check the mechanical room." The warden exited, paused, and did a pirouette. He wrinkled his nose. "What's that smell? Kind of a burnt scent. Guys, check things on the first floor. Sergeant Clark, check the Life Support room. I'll inspect the generator."

Ramsey descended one floor and proceeded along a hall to the mechanical room. The generator purred along. He sniffed. *Same smell, but no smoke? Low tide?*

"Hmm." Something was wrong. Something else? *A different pitch. The generator?* He looked at the air intake fan. The intake stood wide open, but it never ran wide open. *Why?* The warden opened a drawer, found an oxygen meter, and checked the exhaust stack, but it showed only slightly lower than normal. He paused to catch his breath. *What the . . . But, I'm in good shape.* He looked up at one of the building's HVAC air supply vents. *Could it be high carbon monoxide? What would be the source? Maybe carbon dioxide.*

He tore into the supply cabinet and found the meter.

"Shit!" Its membrane dried out long ago. He got the probe kit and hurriedly replaced the semipermeable membrane with shaking hands.

Dizzy, arms and legs heavy. Breathing is so hard.

Hail Mary

Ramsey didn't take time to properly calibrate the meter. He turned it on and waved it up near the vent—eight parts per million. Way beyond the atmospheric 0.04 percent. *Why?*

Stepping behind the electrical generator, he examined one of the oxygen separators that fed the inmate sedation pods. *Man, my head hurts . . . oxygen . . . need oxygen.* Ramsey stumbled back to the supply cabinet and found a roll of quarter-inch tubing. Returning to the oxygen separator, he identified a vapor trap that tapped into the main oxygen gas supply. Opening the stopcock, he pushed the tubing onto it, felt the gas flow against his face, and sucked on the tube end. After a minute he felt better. His head cleared and muscles relaxed.

The guys! The inmates!

Ramsey dropped the tube and walked over to the mechanical room's control console. He called up the blood CO_2 for the inmates—way too high. *Why hadn't the system automatically adjusted? First the guards, I have to warn them!* Lightheaded, he strode back to his oxygen supply. He took several deep breaths and returned to the console.

Hitting the intercom, the warden shouted, "All personnel respond. Get to the mechanical room." Ramsey paused, gasping. "Ron, Mike, Raymond. There are high CO_2 levels in the building." Gasp. He listened for a response, but felt the wooziness return. He stumbled back to his oxygen tube. Taking several breaths, he dashed to the console. "Mike! Ron!"

A Hope in Hell

Ring! Ring! Ring! An audible alarm screamed, and red warning lights flashed. The CO_2 levels in the inmates' cells rose dangerously high.

They're all going to die. Two thousand souls on my watch. Thoughts of his pending appointment to Commissioner of the Department of Corrections rolled through his mind . . . his acceptance speech. *"Sedation is the future of incarceration."*

Ramsey stumbled back to his quarter-inch life line, took three deep breaths and turned to the separators. Both of them had to be reprogrammed manually. He set the dials to manual and returned to the console to override the program: Life Support . . . Settings . . . Oxygen Supply . . . Warning: Life Support Systems Require Security Clearance.

Ramsey's head hurt, the CO_2 in his blood pushed the pH lower, his arms became lead, and his chest heaved with rapid huffing. His head nodded, but snapped up again. *Not on my watch.* Ramsey typed in his clearance code, increased the oxygen air mixture, and turned to get back to the life sustaining oxygen tube only thirty feet away. He imagined himself standing, stepping forward, even lunging, falling, crawling . . . but that didn't happen. His legs wouldn't move. His right arm slid off the chair armrest, tried to push off . . . *no strength.* He looked around. *Ironic, I'm going to die. Charon, the gatekeeper, is going to die in hell.*

Ramsey's lips and mucus membranes reddened.

Within a minute, the console showed the inmate's blood CO_2 levels returning to normal. The alarm stopped. They remained safe and sedated as long as the standby generators ran, as long as the fuel lasted.

Jeff Ramsey registered this as he lost consciousness and his head rolled to one side. His body shuddered, but remained upright in the chair, a grim sentinel for the underworld residents who had outlived their keeper.

* * * * *

The maelstrom battered the hospital with insane-force gusts, turning objects into projectiles and prying at the building's structure. Jason pushed into the hallway, determined to reach the supply closet and the portable bottles of oxygen.

The corridor roared, a tempest of debris, dust, and hundred mile-per-hour missiles of sheet rock and building materials. A copy machine tumbled and slid down the hall until it wedged in a corner. Jason slowly crawled along the inner wall. He peered toward the fabled closet at the end of the passage, but couldn't see it through the whirling miasma. His lungs burned, his head ached. *I won't make it.* Jason struggled to his feet and pushed forward like a rugby player in a scrum.

Three, four, five steps . . . he faltered to his knees. *No strength.* Jason felt his head nod . . . blackness. His left hand hit open space. A room? Fighting off the darkness, he crawled inside, made for the center of the back wall and the oxygen supply stub out. No tube, no mask, just a valve. Turning it, he pressed his head against the wall, his lips around the gas nozzle, and sucked in another reprieve from death. *Life so fragile, so dependent*.

Jason again hyperventilated to supersaturate his blood, then noticed the patient in the room. He put his hand on the man's neck, but did not detect a pulse. After a few more gulps of oxygen, he pushed back into the hall. Four more rooms loomed between his position and the end of the corridor. Jason crawled to the next, but the door stood closed. He turned the handle.

Bam! The lever flew out of his hand and door panel slammed back, bending the hinges. Jason winced from the pain in his bruised rib, struggled to his feet, and lurched inside. A man with an amputated leg, thigh still bandaged, lay in the bed, horror in his eyes. Here, the roof remained intact and there were no windows. Somehow, gusts still entered the room and the changing pressures made Jason's ears pop. He stumbled over next to the patient's bed, pulled a coil of tubing with a respirator mask free of the wall, turned the valve, and inhaled. Looking at the patient's valve setting, he surmised the man had turned the flow of O_2 up himself.

"What the hell's going on? Where's the staff?" the patient shouted.

The psychologist reached out and patted the man's shoulder.

"Are you a doctor?"

Using shouts and sign language, Jason told him to remain there, hang onto the respirator, and it might be the next day before help arrived. Jason tweaked the man's valve open even more. No worries of oxygen toxicity in the short term.

Jason found more blankets and covered the patient. He hyperventilated with oxygen again, pushed back into the hallway, and tried to close the door behind him. After several attempts, he waited. The wind eased, and Jason slammed it shut.

Moving to the next room, he held the door handle tight, eased it open, slipped through, and closed it behind him.

A young male lay in bed with a cast over the lower half of his body. The teenager was unconscious, an oxygen mask over his face, but showed obvious signs of distress. Jason seized the second set of tubing and mask for himself, and turned the gas volume up for the young man. Soon the teenager's eyes flickered. He looked at Jason, bolted upright, and screamed with pain. Terrified he clutched at Jason.

"I couldn't breathe. What's happening?" The young man pleaded for reassurance.

Jason calmed him, told him there was no one to help until morning, and showed him how to adjust the oxygen flow.

The psychologist made his way to the next couple of rooms to take in oxygen, but the patients had already expired. Jason reentered the maelstrom in the hallway, crawled to the end, and found the closet. Standing, he braced himself, waited for a lull, pulled the door open, and slipped inside. *Bam!* The door banged shut. Darkness.

Shit. His lungs ached, head hurt, dizzy. Fumbling for his phone, he turned it on and used it for light. Where're the damn bottles? He rushed over and threw open a cabinet. Nothing. He stepped back, searching. There! Under the cupboards. Jason yanked one out, turned the valve, and sucked on the nozzle, for now, the teat of life itself.

Jason sat in the dark, rested, and recovered his strength. After a few moments, he took inventory. He found all the bottles, tubes, and facemasks they needed. Jason found a flashlight and stuck it in his pocket. Stacking two bottle carts atop another one, he strapped them together. He placed his hand on the door lever with dread. *That wind is going to kick my ass. Gotta get back to Emily.* Jason put his shoulder to the door and forced it open.

He stayed upright as he dragged the oxygen cart-trolley behind him. *Boom!* The whole wing shuddered. A sudden gust lifted the trolley and sent it skidding across the hall, yanking his respirator off. A flying piece of sheetrock hit Jason in the chest, knocking him to the floor. He lay on his back flailing. *Is this it? Pills . . .* Jason wasn't sure if the pain in his chest was from the impact, his bruised ribs, or a new heart attack. No difference, he couldn't reach the pills anyway. Another moment and the pain subsided. *Not a heart attack.*

Something hit his leg and he let out a groan. He looked down. The oxygen trolley, tossed to and fro by the changing winds, rolled onto his legs. He reached for the regulator, pulled at the tubing until he clutched the respirator to his mouth. Catching his breath, he returned to inching his way back up the corridor.

Hail Mary

Jason hated moral choices. He had checked all five rooms on the left side of the hall and found two people still alive. With plenty of portable oxygen, he didn't need to enter the rooms along the right side of the corridor. Like that teenage boy, they may still be alive, but Emily and Anna?

Jason reached the first room. *Damn. Gotta check.* He pushed in and found a slightly older man hugging a heart pillow. Jason guessed he had undergone by-pass surgery. The man could barely open his eyes. He cranked up the oxygen flow, and the patient's respiration smoothed out.

Jason found two more patients still alive. After turning up their gas flow, they regained consciousness. He showed each how to control the oxygen, and assured them they would not be forgotten. After the last one, Jason finally turned to the room with Emily, Anna, Mark, and Mrs. Larson. He crawled across the hall pushing the oxygen trolley ahead of him. The air whistled louder here. He stuck his head in . . .

Oh, shit! The entire roof and half the outside wall had torn away, showing the dark roiling storm moving rapidly above the building. *Oh my God, they're gone!*

Chapter VII

The Silent Patrolman

Atmospheric scientist Bill Johnson was great at chess, Sudoku, science, anything involving left brain, slow-thinking, prowess. He was not good at thinking on his feet. The red and blue flashing lights of the police cruiser started a flood of thoughts: *Run? Explain? Sara and the kids! Shit.* Too many thoughts, too many ramifications. *I'll pay for the damage, storm imminent, we'll all be dead in hours.* So, instead of one clear path of action he wavered between several.

His accomplice, Michael Chennault, ran and jumped into the passenger seat of their car, fully expecting Dr. Johnson to join him and speed away. Bill did not. He took a couple steps toward the driver's side, turned to explain to the police, and then turned again toward the car. The squad car screeched to a stop behind the SUV.

A lone blond-haired officer, jumped out with pistol drawn. "Halt! Halt! Halt!"

Bill turned again, waved his arms, and shouted, "It's alright! An emergency!"

That did little to calm the officer who pointed the weapon at Bill and shouted for the scientist's accomplice to get out of the car.

Bill looked back at Mike and yelled, "Go! Go! Get to my house."

The Frenchman slid over to the driver's side and turned the keys.

The Silent Patrolman

The officer stepped to the left to get a line of fire that included the driver.

Bill held his hands above his head and yelled, "Don't shoot, don't shoot, don't shoot!" As Mike sped off, the policeman aimed, but Bill stepped directly between the two.

"Get on the ground! All the way down. On your stomach." The officer brandished his nine-millimeter Glock.

Bill complied, but craned his neck to read the name on the policeman's uniform. "Officer Meyer, I can explain."

The policeman tapped the communicator on his chest. "Dispatch, did the video get a license plate?"

"Yes, sir," a female voice issued from a collar vid-card. "An eight-forty-two in progress. Officer on the scene. One suspect in custody. Another in a white SUV, license plate Gov, LMR8562. Backup in route, ETA five minutes."

"Jenny? Didn't know you were on duty." He planted a knee in the small of Bill's back. Yanking the scientist's hands behind him, the officer snapped restraints on Bill's wrists with practiced efficiency. "Anyone inside? Who drove off? Where's he going?"

"I'm Doctor Johnson of the National Oceanic and Atmospheric Administration. I can explain—"

"I said, is anyone inside?" The patrolman roughly hauled him to his feet.

"No, there's no one inside," Bill managed to verbalize as the officer pushed him toward the squad car.

"How about your friend with the car? Who is he?"

"That's not important."

"I'll decide that. Now, who are you?"

"I'm Dr. Bill Johnson with—"

"Johnson, Smith, Bill. You guys don't have much imagination. You should try a Wilbur or Leonard sometime." Officer Meyer spun his captive around and deftly removed his wallet and phone. "Well, you do have a Bill Johnson's driver's license. Dispatch, can you verify an ID for me?" Dave held the license in front of the collar vid-card and then on Bill.

"Standby," the female voice replied.

"Look, there's a big storm coming this way. It'll hit in a couple hours. That's why. . ."

Whirrr, Wheerrrr! Another cruiser pulled up and a Latino officer exited, hand near his service weapon. "Have you checked inside yet?"

"No. He says no one's there. But, his buddy sped off."

The second officer stepped back to his car and pulled out a shotgun. "The traffic video grid is down for repair west of here, so we may lose him."

Bill Johnson breathed a sigh of hope.

"Put him in and let's secure the site." The Latino officer pumped a shell into the chamber.

Officer Meyer opened the back door of his cruiser. "Strange one, he says he's a doctor."

"PhD, Head of the NOAA office in Princeton," Bill spat out as the blond official put a hand on his head and guided him toward the back seat. He looked at the silent patrolman, and the iron grate that separated the officers and the perps. *I'm going to die in there. Have to do something.* Bill collapsed to the ground and started wheezing.

"What the—" Dave lost his grip on the perp. The second officer stepped over with the butt of his shotgun raised.

Wheeze. "I have COPD." *Gasp.* "I . . . need oxygen." *Wheeze.* "Please . . . over there . . . oxygen."

"Bullshit. He's trying something." The Latino officer brandished the shotgun butt. "Get in the car or you'll wish you had."

Bill continued to pant. "Please . . ." He let out a croupy cough and nodded to the oxygen bottles just inside the garage door. "You don't want a death on your hands." *Wheeze.* "On camera."

A female voice broke in, "Dispatch has confirmation. There's a ninety-six percent positive facial recognition of a Dr. William Johnson, government civil service, head of the Geophysics Fluid Dynamics Laboratory at Princeton University."

Officer Meyer paused. "Jenny, he's on the ground wheezing. Claims he has COPD and needs oxygen. Please advise."

The female dispatcher snapped back, "For shit sake, Dave. You're not a doctor. If there are signs of him not getting air, give him his inhaler."

The patrolman looked down. "Do you have an inhaler?"

Bill continued to cough. "No." *Huff.* "Need oxygen."

Officer Meyer walked over to the garage. "Damn. He's got me stealing for him." He rolled a bottle over and placed the respirator over Bill's nose and mouth.

The scientist took in several breaths and nodded.

The patrolman helped him to his feet, slid the scientist into the back of the cruiser, and set the oxygen bottle on the floor.

"Hey, I may need to turn the gas up." Bill pointed with his chin and wiggled his arm.

Officer Meyer studied him, glanced at the "silent patrolman" safety screen separating the front and back seat, and reached in to unlock the cuffs. "Okay, but no bon bons." He stepped away, slamming the door.

It took two hours for the owner to show up, and for Dave Meyer and the other officer to document the crime scene and list the missing property. Dark clouds moved in and light winds scattered garbage along the alleyway. The smell of ozone lent the air a pre-storm gloom. The store manager shot Bill a hard stare through the cruiser's rear window, but didn't talk directly with him.

Officer Meyer finally slid behind the driver's seat.

Bill pleaded though the respirator, "Look up at the sky. I just came from the Princeton lab. I've seen the satellite feeds."

Ring. Ring. Ring. Bill's cell phone vibrated in the front seat. "Shit. That's the president's chief of staff. I need to get that."

Officer Meyer glanced in the rear-view mirror. "Shut the hell up." He started the car and drove up the alley.

"Damn it! We have to get warnings out. There's high carbon dioxide gas inside the storm front. It's already hit the West Coast. Don't you understand?"

"I knew you was fakin' it." As Dave pulled onto the main street, rain splatted the windshield and trees swayed in the headlights. "So, you guys are some kind of cult. End of times thing?"

"I know it sounds crazy. I pray I'm wrong. Please take me to my family. You have all my information. I'm not going to run anywhere."

"Sorry. I'm a go-by-the-book guy."

"You have family?" Bill received a stony stare. "If you do, you have to save them."

"Let me guess. A space ship is coming down to save the believers." The officer shook his head. *Whoom!* A gust of wind hit the vehicle. "Whoa! That is coming fast. Enough talk, better get you to the station."

By the time the dedicated patrolman steered the cruiser onto the highway entrance ramp, variable winds forced the cars to creep along at thirty miles-per-hour.

"All-points bulletin, category five storm, Cassandra, is moving in from the coast," the same female dispatcher announced over the officer's comm. "One-hundred-fifty-knot winds are expected. All on-duty personnel are to return to their duty stations. Repeat, all personnel are to return to their duty stations."

"Well, you're right about the storm part." The officer held a white-knuckle grip on the steering wheel as he exited the freeway.

"That's what I'm telling you. We don't get category five storms this far inland." Bill looked nervously outside.

"The station's not far." He drove through the night streets amid tumbling debris. His voice now unsure, "Ooohweee. Smells like hell. What is that?" He breathed in rapid shallow breaths.

"Sulfur compounds, ocean bottom. Holy shit," his voice quavered.

They pulled into the back of the station house. Wind whistled around the vehicle's windows. Bill watched as two other officers got out of their cars, braced against the wind, and fought their way toward the building. One made it inside the station, but the other fell. Bill reached down and turned up his O_2 regulator.

Dave's chest swelled, taking in deeper and deeper breaths. He put his hand on the door lever.

Bill shouted, "Wait!" He nodded at the downed officer.

Officer Meyer looked up and watched as the man tried to get up, staggered, and fell again. "Crap. What's wrong with him?" He opened the front car door and a gust ripped it from his grip, shearing the door hinges and sending it skidding across the parking lot.

"Wait! Unlock my door. Unlock the damn door!" Bill screamed through the respirator over his nose and mouth.

The skeptical official stepped out into the maelstrom, spun, and half fell back inside the car. His chest heaving, he lay with his head on the seat. Rising up, he looked back at his passenger, mystified. His lips cherry red, he reached for the rear door unlock button . . .

* * * * *

94

The Silent Patrolman

Emily and Anna huddled inside the room with their backs to the wind. Mrs. Larson breathed through one of the room's two oxygen systems, while Emily and Anna shared the other. Mark used the portable bottle, but Emily wondered how long it would last. The wind funneled through the doorway and out the open roof with all the force of a jet engine. She raised her head. The hole in the ceiling increased as bits and pieces tore away.

Emily checked on Mark, who appeared to recover from the impact with the door. He rose to his knees, tapped the nurse's shoulder, and pointed toward the hall.

The maintenance man screamed into her ear, "We can't stay here. Stairwell. Get to the stairwell, then the basement."

Emily pointed to her oxygen tube and shrugged.

He held up a finger. He crawled to his tool bag, rummaged around, and pulled out a wrench and a plumbing fitting. He removed the tubing to Emily's and Anna's respirator from the wall, attached it to the portable bottle, and opened the valve. The maintenance man gave a thumbs-up and headed toward the hall.

Emily hesitated. She glanced back at Mrs. Larson, and tugged on the Mark's tubing. He turned and the nurse pointed at the heavy-set patient. The long-haired maintenance man shook his head, drew a finger across his throat, and resumed crawling. Emily clambered back, grabbed the patient's arm and pulled . . . the woman barely moved an inch.

Emily felt a hand on her shoulder. Mark pushed her aside and hooked his arms under the elderly woman. Emily and Anna pushed, and three of them slid the patient along a foot at a time until they reached the end of the fixed tubing. Mark removed it, and they continued, Mark buddy breathing with the patient, and Emily and Anna sharing a respirator.

They pushed into the hallway and the teeth of the tempest. Mark led, dragging Mrs. Larson. Emily and Anna followed. The debris load slowed, fewer flying glass shards, but paper and flying building materials forced them to keep their heads down. At times, the wind nearly lifted Anna off her knees, forcing Emily to keep an arm around her daughter.

They inched along against the gale for what seemed like forever. Every couple of minutes, Mark paused and placed his respirator over Mrs. Larson. He waited to see her breathing even out, took back the respirator, and resumed scooting. They pushed past E-wing and reached the central hall. The wind was even stronger.

Boom! Something shook the building. *Was that the roof?* Emily held Anna tighter.

Mark pointed around the corner to the stairwell sixty feet away. "Lock arms."

He laid the oxygen bottle atop Mrs. Larson and put his arms around her and the bottle. Emily took two deep breaths, passed the respirator to her daughter, then hugged Anna with one hand and gripped Mark's tool belt with the other. The maintenance man kicked off the wall into the funnel of the central hall. The gale tore at them, providing a wind assist, and with little effort they slid along the floor toward the stairwell. As they neared the stairwell door, Mark reached up and grabbed the door's lever, stopping their slide.

Emily held her grip on Mark's tool belt, but they tumbled, and the twisting motion wrenched Anna's arm from her. Anna plunged down the hall toward its intersection with D-wing and the large broken-out, floor-to-ceiling windows at the end of the hall.

* * * * *

Jason's stomach balled up with a hollow ache as if it were the center of his grief-stricken consciousness. *Could they have survived being blown out onto the hospital grounds? From two stories up? Impossible.* He turned back to the E-wing and started for the nearest secure room. *Should he try to look for them?* He could jump out the opening and follow. Stupid idea. *He could . . . could . . . nothing.* But, maybe Emily still had the O_2 bottle. The psychologist stopped. *Why not? He was a walking dead man anyway.*

Almost involuntarily, Jason turned again and crawled resolutely into the room, dragging himself and the oxygen cart toward the howling open gap. No more higher thought processes, almost reptilian, he mechanically pushed to the edge, put one foot over what remained of the broken second-floor wall, grabbed the strap around the oxygen cart, gripped a piece of exposed rebar, and swung himself over and into the darkness, the cart tumbling behind him.

* * * * *

Emily gasped in horror as her daughter tumbled down the hallway toward the broken-out windows and sure death. She looked up at Mark, who hung on for his life. She looked back and let go, sailing toward Anna. The teenager slammed against a support stanchion. She held on for a few seconds as Emily guided her pathway to intersect with her daughter.

Whoop! She hit Anna and wrapped her arms around her. The impact broke the stanchion and the two women swept out the window.

"Aiieeee!" Emily screamed as she plunged into the night.

* * * * *

Jason dangled from the rebar for only a second. It bent. His grip slipping, he dropped twelve feet into a hedge of holly. Scratched and gouged, but surprisingly alive, he repositioned the respirator on his face and crawled from the brush, dragging the banged-up, but functional, oxygen cart with him.

The tempest lessened in the lee of the building. He stood, pulled the flashlight from his pocket, and began searching the grounds.

"Aiieeee!" A muffled scream came from the gloom. *Where? Left, right?* He turned left, marching along the hedge with his flashlight, sweeping the ground with his back to the building as he peered through the dark.

The Silent Patrolman

Whoomph! Something behind him? *What the . . .* The psychologist swung his flashlight around. *Emily! My God. How?* She lay on the ground, half unconscious. Jason quickly slid a respirator over her face and turned up the oxygen. Emily raised an arm. He pointed the flashlight in the direction she indicated. Someone lay stuck in the hedge.

Reaching up, he grabbed Anna and pulled her down. He put his respirator on the teenager and quickly untangled another for himself. Jason put his finger on her neck. She coughed, her chest heaved.

She's alive!

Emily sat up, lifted Anna to a sitting position, and pointed to the closest personnel door. They stumbled to the entrance. Jason held the light as she punched in a code, the lock clicked, and they entered the basement. He shouldered the door closed.

Calm, blessed calm. Even the sounds of Cassandra abated here, an island of sanity in an insane world. Jason slumped to his knees, exhausted.

A moment later, Jason led Emily and Anna toward the noise of the generators. Emergency lighting from the mechanical room spilled into the corridor, but the beam of another flashlight bounced up the hallway. Mark lumbered toward them, pulling Mrs. Larson along.

Jason tried to help as Mark rigged several tap-offs on the supply side of the oxygen separator. He ran long tubes extending just outside the mechanical room where they set up camp with blankets and pillows. Emily tended to Mrs. Larson, who somehow survived the trip.

Mark looked on. "She's a tough old bird, had to drag her down the steps."

Emily took her pulse. "She's okay. You did well. She'll need an IV and some fluid, but it can wait till morning." Anna lay curled up, covered with blankets. Jason glugged water they found in a break-room farther up the basement corridor.

"How about the patients we left upstairs?" Jason, drained of energy, knew he was in no shape to retrieve them.

"They have oxygen supplies as long as we keep this generator and the O$_2$ separator running. We'll have to get them in the morning." Mark looked back at the generator. "It's running rough. Let's hope it holds." He pointed to the entrance of the loading dock. "We keep two liquid oxygen cylinders for backup if need be. I can seal off this entire hallway and supply enough oxygen to breathe without respirators tomorrow."

Jason slid down onto the blankets, closed his eyes, and slept.

* * * * *

Bill banged on the silent patrolman and screamed. A waste of energy. Officer Meyer lay unconscious, and his body began to tremor due to lack of oxygen.

Bill flipped to his side and kicked at the window. No results. He took a deep breath and paused. *What do I have? Take inventory.* Nothing in his pockets . . . *emptied during the arrest. The oxygen cylinder!* Maybe he could bash the window out. He examined the glass, bulletproof? On a fluke, he reached down and pulled the handle. It opened.

Small favors! Thank you, Officer Meyer. Dr. Johnson braced himself, eased the door open and, with the oxygen bottle tucked under his arm, pushed out into the wind.

Wham! Something struck the back of the car and moved it. *If that had hit me?* Bill crawled forward and dove into the front seat atop Officer Meyer, whose body convulsed.

He's alive! Bill slipped his respirator off and held it over the officer's face. He counted to ten, took a couple breaths from the mask and put it back.

One, two, three . . . ten. Still nothing. Again. One, two, three, four . . . Meyer's chest shuddered and heaved. His eyes blinked.

The officer raised his head, glassy eyed and groggy. Bill pushed him over to the passenger side. After taking three breaths and passing the respirator, Bill started the vehicle and gunned it toward the rear entrance of the building. It bounced up the short steps, crashed through the frame of an already shattered window, and stopped halfway inside.

Dr. Johnson recovered from the collision and reached for the respirator but . . . Officer Meyer scrambled out with the oxygen cylinder, and scuttled through the building's lobby. Bill clamored from the car, chest laboring. Even inside the building, the wind forced him to crawl. In the dim light, he saw the patrolman disappear around a corner. Bill forced himself to his feet and followed, lurching down a hall. A shadow flicked across light emitted from a doorway.

Bill stumbled inside a large windowless room. There, under an emergency light, Officer Meyer bent over an unconscious woman dressed in a police uniform. Bill's lungs burned. He nodded into blackness, then light again. He stumbled, fell to his knees, and sank to the floor.

Chapter VIII

A Lonely Planet

Jason awoke with a tap on his shoulder and Emily leaning above him. "How're you doing, Dr. Adams?"

Jason blinked, lifted his hands, felt the respirator on his face, and took a moment to orient himself. *Oh, yeah. The storm . . . low oxygen.* He jerked up, winced from the bruised rib, and took inventory. *Anna?*

"Anna all right?"

The nurse smiled. "You saved us. More than once." Emily leaned in and gave him a grateful hug.

Her daughter sat against the corridor wall, wrapped in a blanket, her face wraith-like. Jason thought she might be in shock.

"Gross, Mom. Hold off on the obligatory hump till I'm out of ear-shot." Anna stood. "Is there any damn food around this place?"

Apparently not in shock, after all.

"There's food in the break room, honey. Mark already, ahh . . . opened the vending machine." Emily stood, removed her respirator and picked up the dual respirators attached to one of the oxygen bottles, passing one to Anna. "I'll show you."

They walked down the corridor trailing the two-wheeled oxygen bottle.

Mark came over. He nodded toward the exterior doors. "The storm's blown itself out, still as death out there. But, what the hell happened last night? I never expected to see those two women again."

"I'm not sure. I came back from the supply closet. The room's wall and roof were gone and nobody there."

"Yeah. We decided to get the hell out of there. Looks like I made a good decision." Mark tapped his chest.

"I thought you'd been blown out, so I went looking. I dropped down, landed in some bushes." Jason inspected some of his cuts and scratches. "I was searching the grounds. Emily landed right behind me."

"Wow! Talk about a needle in a haystack."

Jason tried to stand, but winced as his sore ribs bit into his side. Mark helped him up. "You're banged up a bit?"

"Rough night. Hey, we got patients on the second floor."

"Let's get something to eat first, secure our room, make the air breathable, and then we'll see if they're still . . . there."

Mark ran a one-inch hose from the oxygen separator to the break room and added weather stripping around the door edges. He held up a four-foot square filter. "Lucky! It's good to be green. These carbon filters can work as CO_2 scrubbers." He duct-taped the filter over the vent.

"In an hour or so, that'll lower the CO_2 and build up enough oxygen to breathe inside here."

"Great. We have a sanctuary." Jason slumped into a chair and paused to regain his breath. He felt useless. *No energy, damn heart.*

A Lonely Planet

Emily and Anna returned with an armload of snacks and drinks. The nurse looked Jason over. "Are you taking your meds?"

Jason nodded.

They ate in silence, awkwardly lifting the respirators to take in the vending machine fare. Afterward, the four ambulatory survivors secured fresh oxygen bottles and prepared to head upstairs.

Emily reached over and squeezed Anna's arm. "Honey, you don't have to go. I prefer you stay here. Stay with Mrs. Larson."

"Okay. How long?" Anna finally dropped the attitude and appeared vulnerable.

"A couple hours. We'll be back as soon as we can, sweetie."

Jason followed Mark and Emily, but he paused several times while ascending the stairwell. When they arrived at the second floor, Mark opened the door. His jaw dropped, he paled, and his shoulders slumped. Emily sank to the floor and wept, head buried in her arms.

Jason braced himself, summoned his professional stoic detachment, stepped past Mark and took in the scene. All his experience as a psychologist dealing with the pathos of the human condition failed. His control slipped and his body shook, tears welled and streamed down his checks.

Why . . . why, why, why . . . why did so many bodies end up here? The corridor lay littered with debris as expected, but the *corpses*! Cassandra, as if striving for maximum horror effect, deposited everything weighing between fifty and a hundred kilos right here for their first view of the new world.

Like rubber ducks in a stream, floating and piling up in a particular eddy. Patients lay wrapped around broken beams, piled in corners, impaled on rebar.

Jason bent over and closed his eyes. Several moments passed.

Mark recovered first. "Clean up on aisle planet Earth." His voice sounded disembodied.

Emily tapped Jason's shoulder and took his arm. "Let's find survivors."

He followed her, stepping over debris and bodies, wending their way back to E-wing. Only half of the hospital roof remained, and dark heavy clouds hid the sun. The surface, outside, smelled of low tide and sulfuric compounds. *Rotten eggs, sulfuric acid?*

They passed the room Mrs. Larson had occupied.

Emily opened the next door. A figure lay in the bed. Jason remembered the dead man he had found there.

"No." Jason guided her away.

The next room held the amputee. The poor man nearly bounced out of bed, obviously anxious to see someone, anyone. While Emily assured the patient, Jason slid to the next room with the teenager in the half-body cast.

The young man lay on the floor and looked like a lost puppy. "Help me, please. I tried to crawl out and hurt my leg again," the teenager cried. "Shit. It really hurts. What's going on out there? Nobody came."

A Lonely Planet

"We're here now." Jason checked his pulse. "A nurse is here. She'll give you something."

"I couldn't breathe. I still can't frickin' breathe. Where is everybody."

"It was a bad storm." Somehow, dealing with the boy fortified Jason, put him in functional mode. "Many people, patients and staff, didn't survive. As you found out, the air is anoxic. We have to have supplemental oxygen to stay alive."

Emily stuck her head inside.

Jason turned back. "He needs some pain meds."

"There're some at the nurse's station." Emily mustered a weak smile for the teen. "Hang in there, honey. I'll be right back.

"And, I'll be back with a gurney. We'll get you downstairs. There's a room where you can breathe without a respirator. Better yet, there's a girl your own age down there." He winked at the kid, trying to lighten the mood.

It took two hours to ferry all five patients in E-wing down to the basement break room. Jason had done what he could to prepare them for the horror that lined the upstairs corridor, but a grim pallor hung over the survivors in the aftermath.

They stocked the room with beds, blankets, food, and medicine. Emily stayed to care for the infirm, while Mark and Jason went upstairs to find more survivors.

Mark led the way out of E-wing and down the ramp. Jason rolled a cart of oxygen bottles along behind him. Movement caught his eye. Something, someone was alive.

Jason pulled his respirator away to shout. "Hey! Over here."

The rescuers waved, but saw no response. They wound their way toward an old man. Nude, he wore a respirator and rolled an oxygen bottle. His hospital gown must have been torn away. The man simply stared at them.

"Hello?" Mark waved his hand in front of the man's face. When the patient did not respond, Mark opened his palms, in a questioning gesture. "Is he nutso?"

"He must be in shock." Jason grabbed the man's shoulders. "What's your name?"

The patient said something unintelligible.

Jason shrugged. "He might have dementia or something." The psychologist turned back to the patient. "We're going to take you downstairs. It's safer there. Can you hear me?"

The man nodded with some level of understanding.

Jason checked the patient's oxygen bottle—it indicated near empty. "I better swap this out."

Jason attached a full bottle and started to lead the nude survivor toward the basement.

Mark stopped him with a hand on his arm. "Oh, hell. I'll take him. But, let's find him some pants. This ain't a frickin' octogenarian nudist camp."

Only thirty feet away, Jason found a corpse in blue coveralls. He looked back at Mark.

The maintenance man raised his eyebrows. "Shit. It's Carl."

Jason shrugged.

"Go ahead. I never liked him, anyway."

Jason unzipped the coveralls and yanked them off. He held them out to the old man, who took them and put them on.

As Mark led the man away, Jason said over his shoulder, "I'll be in D-wing."

"Okay. I'll catch up with you there."

Jason hoped infants in the nursery incubators might have survived. On his way there, he paused at C-wing, the hospital's mental health ward.

He entered the reception area. "Hey, anybody here?"

No response.

Part of the roof lay asunder. Several corpses rested among the flotsam and wreckage of mangled tree branches, broken sheetrock, glass shards, and mud.

"Hello! Anyone here?"

Something caught his eye. A young man lay bent over a set of lounge chairs, his back impossibly twisted. Jason stared at a tattoo on the corpse's right hand—a horned snake?

Oh, no! Tyrell must have come to the hospital's grief therapy. Why else would he come here for shelter?

Unreasoned guilt welled up inside Jason.

He would have died anyway. Jason shook off his overwrought contemplation and proceeded to D-wing and the nursery, occasionally shouting, "Anyone here?"

The nursery window, the future.

Jason pressed his face against the glass eyeing each basinet for movement, crying, anything. His heart, already so heavy, now felt even worse. He pined for the son or daughter he never had.

I'd better check, just in case. Jason walked inside and lifted the first blanket, and the next, and the next, and the next . . .

He returned to the hall and sank onto the floor. He sharply inhaled, tried but couldn't exhale, and inhaled again. Soon, his body broke into paroxysms. He continued, unable to stop until a hand shook his shoulder.

"Hey, hey. You're hyperventilating. Stop it." The handyman noticed the basinets, and lifted Jason by the arm. "Come on. Let's get out of here."

"Hello. Hello. Anybody?" Mark led Jason up B-wing and stopped at the first room. "Hello." He looked inside, turned and shook his head.

Jason, working to calm his breathing and to concentrate on what needed to be done, took the rooms on the right. "Coming in," he announced, but the outer wall had blown out, and the room lay empty. "Hey, Mark. Are the O_2 lines in the outer wall? If so, no one along this wing would have had any oxygen."

Mark looked. "Shit. And, we're spilling oxygen here. No wonder the separator was working so hard. Let's hurry and check this corridor, then I can shut it off."

They proceeded to the end of the hall without results.

Jason grimaced. "You can shut off the leak now."

Mark turned off the gas.

In the next wing, they crawled over a tangle of wreckage, office machines, wires, wheelchairs, and tree branches. A dead sparrow hung plastered against one wall, but A-wing stood mostly intact.

Jason tried the first room and found a lifeless young woman.

"Yo! Anybody home. Olly, olly, oxen free," Mark yelled, and stuck his head in the next room.

"Hey! Hey!" A voice sounded from down the corridor.

A middle-aged man stood in the hall, waving. Jason and Mark marched up to him. He carried a portable bottle under one arm and pointed to the adjacent room. "There are four of us. Everyone else is dead."

Inside, two patients reclined in beds and wore respirators connected by tubing to the gas outlets. A third person, a woman in her fifties, sat in a chair dressed in street clothes. Several portable oxygen bottles lay scattered around the room. A gray-haired man let out a whoop and the woman clapped her hands.

At the same time, a young man with his abdomen wrapped in gauze sat up. "It's about time. Where the hell have you been? I pay taxes, God damn it, we've been here all morning."

Jason stared at the boy calmly. "We're not emergency services. We're survivors just like you." The room went silent. "From what I heard on the broadcast, this isn't a local event. It's up and down the west coast."

The older man pulled off his respirator, inhaled, coughed, and quickly put it back on. "What are you saying? The whole area is like this? Can't breathe?"

"We may be talkin' major apocalypse, man." Mark nodded toward the hall. "Lots o' dead people out there."

Jason stepped over and examined the young man. "We don't know the extent. For now, we're on our own. There are nine survivors in the basement. Mark's set up a room so we can breathe inside without respirators. You folks make thirteen. What brought you to the hospital?"

"I had appendicitis. They cut me open." The young man pointed to his wound.

"Okay. We'll get you downstairs." Jason turned to the woman in street clothes. "Are you ambulatory?"

* * * * *

Bill blinked and looked up to see Officer Meyer's tear-streaked face. He held a respirator over the scientist's mouth, took it away, inhaled three quick breaths, and passed it back. Bill sat up, observed the prostrate woman near him and the grieving officer between them, who shook his head.

The scientist squeezed his shoulder, and leaned in to shout over the tempest outside, "I'm sorry!" He paused. "This little bottle won't last. Do they have scuba rescue gear here?"

Slowly, the officer pointed to the hall and to the right.

Bill hustled to the storage room. By the light of his phone, he quickly located the scuba gear, cranked open a tank valve, and sucked on the mouthpiece. Putting the straps on, he pushed back into the hallway and the maelstrom.

Bam! Something struck the building. *A tree?*

A Lonely Planet

He returned to the dispatch room. Officer Meyer still sat, bent over, holding the uniformed woman. Bill checked a couple other policemen who lay on the floor, no movement, no pulse. He knelt down and tried artificial resuscitation on one, counting out the chest compressions. *No response.* He scanned the wall for an emergency defibrillator—nothing. *Yeah, had to make sure.*

He stepped over, sat next to the grieving man, glanced quickly at the name on the patrolman's badge again, and shouted over the storm, "Dave? Your wife?"

Dave shrugged, but continued to stare down at the woman in his arms. He finally looked up. "Yeah."

"The storage room is safer. Come."

The officer stared with vacant eyes.

Bill tried to help him up. "Come on. We'll find survivors when this is over." Dave just sat there. The scientist continued talking, hoping to bring the officer out of his state of shock, "There's lots of air, lots of scuba gear. You'll be needed when . . ." *My family! Did Michael make it? Are they alive?* His heartache returned and a hollowness rose in his chest. *Pull yourself together. One step at a time.*

He helped Dave to his feet, who followed, zombie-like. They pressed themselves into the gale, stumbled along the hall and into the storage room. Bill forced the door closed.

Using the light from his phone, he found blankets. He checked the oxygen level in Dave's tank.

"A couple more hours." He stacked several scuba tanks nearby. Officer Meyer sat in stony silence. Bill started to talk. "In the morning. We'll . . ." He paused. "We'll make a plan."

No response. Bill gave up, locked onto the idea of getting home as soon as the storm abated, and lay down in darkness.

* * * * *

Jason led the four survivors of B-wing to the basement while Mark finished searching the hospital wards. When he arrived, Emily kept busy setting up beds and caring for the patients inside the break room. "Four more. Mark's still searching."

Emily looked the new arrivals over. "No nurses? Doctors?"

Jason shook his head.

"We're running out of room for beds. We can move some tables out." Emily began clearing space. "Anna, honey, can you help Dr. Adams get the beds from level two?"

Anna sat huddled over in a corner and looked on as if she were a tourist in an unpleasant neighborhood. "I'm not going out there. Shit. They can sleep on the tables."

"Anna!" Emily turned to her daughter, disappointed.

Marjorie, the fiftyish woman stood up. "I can help."

"Thank you." Jason checked her O_2 bottle. "You've got plenty of oxygen. The beds are upstairs."

Jason and Marjorie returned with the beds, as Mark arrived with four more elderly patients, which brought the total to seventeen. "I searched all the wards, even the grounds."

Emily paused from changing a colostomy bag and crossed her arms. "Seventeen out of over a thousand, plus four hundred staff. Hard to believe not one medical doctor made it."

"Did you get a look toward downtown? Jason asked.

"A bit. The highway's stock still. Nothing but devastation as far I can see. The skyline doesn't look the same. Couple of the buildings damaged." Mark turned and bumped into a bed jostling the patient. "Sorry, too crowded in here. I'll get this whole floor oxygenated tomorrow."

* * * * *

Bill dozed off a couple times. Each time he woke, Dave sat there, still in shock. The scientist ventured out once to get water and food from a kitchen down the hall. He offered it to the patrolman who shook his head. "At least drink something. You need to hydrate."

The traumatized officer finally took a few sips. Bill checked his scuba tank, 2100 psi, he had only used a third of it. He lay back down and waited for morning.

Dawn brought only dim light, but the storm noise no longer raged outside their closet. *Must have blown over.* Bill roused himself and stood. "I'll check it out."

The grieving officer looked haggard, like he hadn't slept. Bill pushed the door open a crack and crawled out atop four feet of debris. Ten yards down the hall his feet finally found the floor. Outside, the wind still gusted, but only paper, bottles, and dust filled the air. *Almost blown out.* Cars lay jumbled in different reposes as if someone had thrown giant pieces of a board game onto the parking lot. He scanned for one, any car or truck that looked serviceable—an armored truck in the back still sat with its four wheels on the ground. *Dave will know about that.*

The scientist crawled back over the debris pile and stuck his head inside the storage room. "Dave, the storm's almost over. We can get out." He dug at the flotsam to open the door wider. "Start passing me the scuba gear."

The patrolman seemed rooted, but finally got up and handed over eight sets of scuba tanks. He clambered out and stared at the havoc, but didn't speak.

"Dave, there's an armored car in the parking lot. Keys?"

Leading them through office wreckage, the officer paused by the entrance to the dispatch room.

The scientist took the other man's arm, "You don't want to look."

They continued to the front of the building where Dave maneuvered behind a caged station and handed over the keys.

"Does the vehicle have a winch?

His companion nodded.

"Then, let's get loaded up."

A Lonely Planet

Bill took two scuba tanks and headed for the parking lot. He looked back.

Dave waved from the hall. "I'll be right there."

Bill loaded the tanks and started the vehicle. *Yes! Lots of gas.* Checking out the parking lot, he backed up and pointed it toward a rear gate blocked by an overturned squad car. He pulled the cable winch out and hooked it onto the squad car's frame. *No problem. Where the hell is Dave?*

Bill returned to the hall. *No Dave?* He thought the officer might be getting more scuba gear and proceeded to the storage room. *No one?*

Bang! A report echoed off the walls.

Bill numbly walked to the dispatch room—forced himself to look inside. Dave lay atop his significant other, blood oozing on the floor. Even breathing through the snorkel mouthpiece, Bill smelled the gunpowder. The horror of the last twenty-four hours caught up with him. He sank to the floor and wept.

Chapter IX

Lonelier Yet

Jason felt less than useful. Emily was a bulwark, practical and energetic. She held the group together, nursing patients, keeping the focus on the everyday functions of life. His own attempts at grief counseling fell flat. *How can I console others when I can't even come to terms myself?* Additionally, his heart condition sapped his physical energy.

The psychologist mostly followed Mark around and handed him tools. They sealed and oxygenated the entire wing of the basement, so the seventeen survivors spread out into their own rooms. With a little repair, the hospital's emergency systems provided breathable air, food, and water.

Next, Jason watched Mark reprogram the engine on an ambulance to run leaner. They installed CO_2 scrubbers, loaded oxygen cylinders inside the cab, then sealed and chocked the vehicle's vents to prevent leakage. They were mobile. Priority mission: look for other survivors, but the maintenance man made a long list of needed equipment and supplies—a winch for the ambulance, a shortwave radio, and spare parts for the oxygen separator.

Early the second morning, Mark and Jason took off toward downtown Seattle. They periodically honked the horn and scanned for signs of life. The main roads remained passable, but they found the side roads jumbled with wreckage. Everything dead—cats, dogs, birds, and of course people. Mark pointed to smoke columns on the horizon. "Someone left an oven on or a signal fire?"

Jason peered. "That's at least twenty miles."

"I know some shops we can stop at along the way."

Near downtown, they exited onto a side street and wove between wreckage to an industrial park near the port. Jason hit the horn. *Honk! Honk! Honk!* They exited. Mark pointed to a welding supply shop. Most of the cinder block building survived the storm. They entered the dark interior.

Mark shined a flashlight. "Look for a portable welding machine. About so big."

Jason didn't have a flashlight so, again, he felt useless. He walked through a hall and into a garage bay that provided enough light from a small window to make out the tools along a bench. *Got to be a flashlight in a tool chest.* After five minutes of pawing through drawers, he found one. He turned to a backroom that might have been a welding bay.

Clang! Jason jumped out of his skin. *Clang. Clang. Clang.* Somebody was alive. Jason looked out the back. A man stood outside the garage beating a pipe against a metal plate. He dragged a welder's handcart containing both oxygen and acetylene tanks. "Hey, hey, hey. Hello! Anybody here?" *Clang. Clang. Clang.*

Jason stepped out and waved to him. "Here. Right here."

The man lumbered toward him pulling the handcart. "Thank, God. I thought everybody was dead."

As the man threw his arms around Jason and clapped his back, Mark came out.

"I thought—" The man paused to puff on the gas hose attached to his oxygen bottle. Seeing Mark, he went over and slapped his shoulder, then Jason's again, as if to make sure they were real. "I thought everyone was dead." He slipped to the ground and sucked on the hose.

"Easy, take it easy." Jason bent down and looked at his red swollen eyes. "You may have some oxygen toxicity. Let's get you inside the ambulance." Jason led him through the shop and out to the vehicle. "What's your name?"

"Ryan. I couldn't sleep. Every time I dozed off the hose fell out of my mouth."

"You'll do better in the ambulance. We have the basement of Sisters of Mercy Hospital set up for survivors."

Jason helped Mark load a cutting torch and a portable welder in the back of the ambulance. The psychologist slipped into the driver's side and stepped in the back to check on Ryan. His eyes looked better already.

Jason returned to the interstate and drove north toward the fires. They made two more stops to pick up an electric winch, and a shortwave receiver-transmitter. By the time they stopped at the first fire, Ryan had fallen asleep in the back. They drove into a suburban neighborhood. Half of the homes lay heavily damaged, some with only a few walls standing. They followed the smoke to a smoldering house.

Few flames. Low oxygen? Jason honked the horn, exited, and looked around.

Mark cracked the ambulance window and yelled, "Nothing, man! Let's get out of here."

"One minute." Jason crossed to a neighboring house.

"Hey, you don't wanna' go in there," Mark entreated.

Jason proceeded and entered the house. "Hello." *If anyone's here they'd be in the basement.* Something pushed him on, something that demanded witness. He found the stairs and descended. Smelling death, he paused. He had to look. Shining a light around, he found the family huddled on a couch in one corner. Mother, father, four kids of various ages—six corpses, six mouths stretched agape in silent screams. *All hyperventilated until they lost consciousness.* He examined each face. *Why? Why? Why?* The saddened psychologist returned to the vehicle.

Mark sat impatiently. Jason's face betrayed his mood. "I told you," Mark said with a gravelly voice, his tone void of its usual dark sarcasm.

Jason started the ambulance. "Let's forget the other fires for now. Virginia Mason Hospital is on the way back. That may be our best chance of finding survivors."

"Yeah, but it's likely they'll be old, feeble, and near dead."

Jason glared at Mark.

"Whatever. I'm just sayin', it's gonna take more able bodies than what we have so far to survive."

A Hope in Hell

Virginia Mason looked even worse than Sisters of Mercy. Ryan stayed in the vehicle, while Jason and Mark crawled through the ruins. Mark had found air horns at a sporting goods store. Occasionally they blared them as they walked through the wreck. *Honnnk. Honnnk.* The pair split up, each taking a wing. *Honnnk.*

Jason arrived at the end and tried to enter the basement, but debris completely blocked the stairwell. Through a broken glass panel, he lowered himself outside and looked for a ground-level basement door or window. He finally came to the rear of the building and found a loading ramp with a personnel doorway that looked open. *The door might have blown off.* As he got closer, he saw plastic sheeting taped to the opening. Someone had done that! *Honnnk. Honnnk.* Jason laid on his air horn and entered the basement.

Ding, Ding, Ding, came from down the corridor. Jason shouted. "Hello! Hello!"

He received an answer. "Help! We're here. We're here!"

* * * * *

Bill finally got over his grief-driven paralysis. *I have to get to Janice, to my family.* He finished loading the armored truck, yanked the squad car out of the way, and headed for home.

It took four hours to go twenty miles, stopping to winch trees, vehicles, and steel girders out of his path. He exited the freeway next to a mall only two miles from his suburban home. Several vehicles blocked the exit ramp. Bill got out, shouldered his scuba tank, and pulled the winch's cable free. The scientist avoided looking inside the cars. He'd seen enough slumped-over corpses. As he knelt down to hook the winch to one of the blocking vehicles, the rattle of shopping cart wheels caught his attention. A man and a woman ran across the mall's parking lot pushing a cart packed with goods. Bill waved and shouted.

They each breathed from a portable oxygen bottle. They did not answer, but kept pushing the cart and jogging toward him. When they drew near, the content of their carts made him apprehensive— food, water, extra oxygen bottles, and rifles on top.

"Hey, I knew there would be survivors. I got plenty of scuba gear."

When they didn't acknowledge, Bill edged back toward the armored vehicle. The man abandoned the cart and shouldered the assault rifle. Bill sprinted for the truck.

Pow, Pow, Pow! Bullets ripped the pavement in front of him, and he pulled up short.

"Stop right there!" The gray-haired man pointed the weapon at Bill's chest. "Honey, git up there see what's in that truck." A middle-aged woman, carrying a shotgun, hustled up to the armored vehicle.

"Check inside. Go on. I got 'em covered." The man with the rifle approached.

The woman turned and stuck her head inside the vehicle.

Bill stood dumbfounded. *These people are straight out of an old Hollywood movie.* "There's plenty of air. Lots of scuba tanks. Put the gun down. No need—"

"Halleluiah, praise be, he's got tanks and tanks in 'ere." The woman turned around and held the shotgun on Bill.

"Are the keys in there?" the old man yelled.

"Yeah, hon. Git the shoppin' cart. I got 'im covered."

As they loaded their stuff into the vehicle, Bill remembered the bottle on his back was near empty. "There's plenty of air for everyone. We have to stick together." That fell on deaf ears. "I'm Bill Johnson. I'm a scientist . . . trying to get back to my family." The woman got inside the passenger door. "They're only a couple miles from here," Bill pleaded. The man slid into the driver's seat, but still held the gun on him. Bill stepped toward them. "Hey, come on, I'm almost out of air—"

"I killed a man for this here bottle, an' one mo' don't make me no difference." He started the car.

The woman yelled. "Don't mean to be bad. The only people gonna survive this is the ones with guns and air. Good luck to ya." The armored car backed up, turned around, and sped off, dragging the winch cable.

Idiots. Bill shook his head. *Of all the people to survive.* He checked his scuba tank. *Three hundred pounds, less than an hour.* Bill strode in the direction of his house, looking for a car with keys and gas. He finally found one, but had to pull two corpses out first.

Weaving between rubble, he drove within a hundred yards of his house where several trees blocked the way. Bill blasted the horn and started to walk when the scuba hose made a glugging sound. *Shit, out of air!* He sucked harder, but got less. He marched forward and tried to breath. Nothing. But, the government SUV sat in the driveway. *Michael made it.* His family survived!

Bill's chest ached. He fell to his knees and pulled the tank off. Worthless now. He struggled to his feet, his muscles trembling. *I won't make it.* He fell right back down. Blackness, light. *The tank! The tank. . . divers have a reserve supply.* He reached back, fumbled with the regulator controls and found the reserve lever. *Whoosh.* Air rushed through the mouthpiece. He managed to put it into his mouth.

After several breaths, he became aware of a distant sound . . . *thump, thump, thump.* Bill got to his feet and staggered toward the house. *Whop, whop, whop, whop.* The rhythmic sound got louder and louder. The door opened and Michael stepped out, followed by Janice.

Whoosh. Air, dust, and debris rushed around him. *What the* . . . A military helicopter landed in the street. Two soldiers exited the aircraft and ran forward, assault rifles in ready position. A man in a suit followed behind the soldiers.

Bill pushed against the downwash and stumbled ahead as his wife ran toward him. He grabbed Janice in his arms, and they kissed between brief pauses for air. The stress of the last twenty-four hours melted with a rush of euphoria.

The euphoria didn't last long. The man in the suit stood a few feet away. "Bill Johnson, I'm Chief-of-Staff Gerald Sullivan. Under martial law, by order of the president of the United States, you are to come with us.

* * * * *

Jason stood on the roof, feeding out wire to Mark as the maintenance man climbed a jury-rigged antenna tower.

"Hey, gimme some slack," Mark barked as he held on with one arm and tried to pull the wire with the other.

"It's slack down here." Jason stepped sideways and looked up. "Damn, it's hung up on something. Hold tight, I'm going to yank it loose." Jason whipped the coaxial cable pulling it free of the tower crossbar.

"Watch it. You almost jerked it out of my hand," Mark groused. "I ain't climbing up here again."

Setting up the antenna for the shortwave radio marked the next step in a long list of survival tasks: air, water, food, sanitation, find survivors, and connect with the rest of the world, if a rest-of-the-world still existed.

Mark had previously set a strobe atop the hospital roof to attract any wanderers. Several people drifted in the first few nights, but the numbers followed the law of diminishing returns. By the fifth day, no more arrived. The Sisters-of-Mercy compound swelled to fifty-two survivors, but only thirteen able bodies.

Though old technology, the shortwave radio might be the only thing that could work with the satellite systems not functioning. "That should do it." He made the last connection and shimmied down. "Let's go see if anyone's out there."

The two returned to the basement through a door sealed against air leakage. Mark had set up a tool shop across from the generator room. Coaxial cable tacked along the walls led to a bench in one corner of the shop, which connected to a radio transmitter. Half of the compound gathered around as they prepared to turn it on.

One lady pressed her hands together and stared at the radio. "Somebody somewhere will have survived. God will answer us. I know he will."

"Let's hope He's got a short-wave radio," Mark reached over and turned the receiver on. Nothing but loud static came over the speakers. Mark passed the microphone to Jason. "Hell, I don't know what to say."

Jason shrugged. "Hello, hello. We are survivors at Sisters-of-Mercy Hospital in Seattle, Washington . . . Hello? Hello?" Jason waited. "We are survivors in Seattle, Washington. We will check this frequency daily at twelve noon."

Mark turned to another frequency and Jason announced again. The psychologist waited. "We are survivors in Seattle, Washington. We will check this frequency daily at twelve noon."

They tried a few more before most people got bored and left the room. Mark started dialing through the frequency range. *Hissss. Hissss. Hissss.* He found only noise. *Hissss. Hissss.* The remaining few audience members kept silent, but exuded disappointment.

Jason offered, "We'll set a monitoring detail to run the radio every day. It takes a while to get stuff like this set up. There's got to be someone out there."

* * * * *

Hell's Gate Prison weathered the storm as designed. Structurally, the building stood untouched. Even its fences stayed intact. Other than downed trees and debris scattered across the yard, the prison remained a picture of pastoral repose. Its hazardous holdings of pedophiles, rapists, murderers, and offenders with a rainbow of psychotic disorders continued to slumber without regard to the dead guards scattered here and there throughout the prison, without regard to Warden Jeff Ramsey's corpse sitting sentinel-like in the mechanical room control chair.

Ironically, the prison builders designed it like the mythical Pandora's Box—the box that held all the evils of the world, but with one saving grace: "hope" lay stored steadfastly at the bottom. Males made up more than ninety percent of the prison population and occupied the upper levels of its nine subterranean floors—subfloors two through eight. Subfloor nine held the fairer sex. They were still murderers, prostitutes, and embezzlers, and they sported an even wider range of psychotic disorders than the men, but therein lay hope, remote non-perfect hope for a future, a future that included human beings, *Homo sapiens sapiens*.

Lonelier Yet

Whooomph. The hum of the generator dropped in pitch, the lights shut off, and building fans stopped. The fuel tanks held less than 300 gallons—the designed-in shutdown for all nonessential loads meant to conserve fuel for the life-support systems. Shutting down the ventilation allowed the gases from the dead guards, gases of decomposition, putrescine and cadaverine, to fill the corridors of Hell's Gate, adding an even more macabre ambience. But, by lowering the load, the generators, oxygen separators, and sedation and nutrient pumps would continue for another three days.

Chapter X

The Big Fart

The nicely appointed conference room held an oak table, cushioned arm chairs, 3D viewing screens, even a well-stocked refrigerator, but no windows, because it lay two thousand feet below ground. Cheyenne Mountain was built to withstand thermonuclear war, but more importantly it operated on its own air supply system.

Six men shuffled papers and tapped electronic tablets, only occasionally looking up at the man who called them together. Chief of Staff Gerald Sullivan filled-in for the president's science advisor, who remained missing and presumed dead, a casualty of the Great H-B.

New names for the apocalypse surfaced every day but H-B, short for Holocene Barrier, became the favorite for the scientists. Doomsday, Apocalypse, End of Times, The Great Extinction, Gotterdammerrung, Ragnarok, even the most common favorite among the younger crowd—The Big Fart—wasn't used by the scientific brain trust. The extinction that claimed 99.99999985 percent of the human population would be officially called The Great H-B. Some people inside the Mountain didn't like the use of the word "barrier," since it connotes the end of something. But, Earth's geologic time periods were demarcated by major changes in Earth's biosphere: the P-T Barrier (Permian–Triassic), marking the end of the age of amphibians; the K-T Barrier (Cretaceous-Paleogene), marking the end of the age of dinosaurs; and now the Great H-B (Holocene Barrier), marking the end of the . . . age of man?

Bill Johnson put on a collared shirt, but skipped the tie. The other scientists came as is. No one dressed more than functionally within the mountain bunker except the president's cabinet. That included Gerald Sullivan in a three-thousand dollar suit and a fresh haircut. Bill resented him. *He didn't send warnings out in time to save anybody except the president. With no science background, how the hell is the guy going to save the damn world?*

Beep. Beep. Gerald answered his phone and looked up. "Gentlemen, President Meacham will be here in a moment.

Bill leaned over to Dr. Jean Girard and pointed to his tablet. "I can't say anything about this without new satellite data."

"Then we must reconnect to les satellites. We must convince him that—"

The door opened, a secret service agent stepped in with a Glock in a shoulder holster. He surveyed the room and nodded. The looming six-foot-four-inch president strode in.

Gerald stood. "Gentlemen, you are now officially the president's science team, under emergency order forty-two, section six—"

Meacham sat down and spoke gruffly, interrupting his chief of staff. "Please tell me what I need to know briefly and to the point. I need the big picture without a bunch of techno mumbo jumbo. Now, who the hell is Bill Johnson?"

Bill cleared his throat and raised a hand.

"What the hell happened, and will this planet ever support human life again?"

Bill sat taken aback. "All the theories didn't predict this, except . . ." He turned to the Frenchman. "Jean Girard's theory, at this point seems to be the closest to explaining what's happened."

Girard took over. "My theory rests on two sources of gases. Volcanic sources released a large amount of carbon dioxide, smaller amounts of sulfur dioxide, hydrogen sulfide, methane, and helium. But, the volcanic sources alone could not have done this. We think they initiated a massive release of oceanic carbon and methane stores—methane clathrates, hydrates, benthic ooze, mid-ocean organic carbon sinks. Volumes . . . ahh . . . total mass of these—"

"Okay, okay. So, regardless of where they came from, these gases killed everyone who breathed them."

One of the other gentlemen interjected, "Actually, the gases weren't caustic, or poisonous. People and animals died of hypercapnia, high CO_2 levels. They simply suffocated."

The president pointed up. "This cloud cover is a part of this whole damn thing?"

Bill reentered the conversation. "Yes. It appears the cloud cover is caused by a planet-wide temperature inversion. We think . . . I think it's holding the released gases in the lower troposphere. But, if the entire atmosphere mixed top to bottom, then volumes of anoxic gas would dissipate enough. The air would be breathable again."

The Big Fart

"*S'il vous plait, Monsieur Presidente*, to confirm, we must access satellite data from the Kennedy Space Center," Girard interjected.

Meacham furrowed his eyebrows.

Sullivan jumped in. "Sir, summer temperatures may remix the atmosphere and make the air breathable again. Somebody needs to go to Florida and try to access weather satellite data."

"Damn it! I'm not an idiot. I know what he said. But, we're spread a little thin, if you haven't noticed. What I cannot spare are pilots, aircraft, and manpower. Summer will save us or not, with or without the satellite data." President Meacham cleared his throat. "Now, the biologists. Which one of you is Carl Waisanen?"

Bill's heart sank. At the end of the table a large man, mid-forties, full head of blond hair, raised his hand. "Sir."

"You're telling me a near complete apocalypse, toxic air, and straining oxygen generators is not enough, that I gotta worry about goddamn genetics!"

Waisanen hunched forward. "Ahh . . . uh. Yes, Mr. President." He looked down at his tablet. "We have confirmed only one thousand, four hundred twenty-seven people scattered in twenty-some locations. Far apart, some are only one or two individuals. The largest outside of here, is two hundred-and-some in Russia. So far, it's been the law of diminishing returns, fewer and fewer new survivors discovered per day. It's unlikely we will exceed two thousand or even eighteen hundred. Many of the survivors are elderly or infirm. We've identified the reproductive aged females, roughly one hundred and thirty-seven. As we unfortunately experienced yesterday, suicide has taken a toll on—"

"Get to the point, dammit!" President Meacham barked.

"The next generation will be fewer than this one, the lack of genetic diversity will affect fitness, and subsequent generations may continue to decline. Even with frozen embryos, if we can get them, we need women with wombs to make a human being. Bottom line, we need a minimum of four hundred reproducing females for humanity to survive beyond the short term."

"So, we need some baby-making machines." President Meacham turned to Gerald Sullivan. "I wanted to keep hookers in the White House basement just like Kennedy did, but no, you advised against it, said it wouldn't be politically correct. So, I was right again."

"Circumstances change, Mr. President," Sullivan acknowledged. A couple people smirked, but most sat grim faced. He stepped in again. "What I believe Waisanen and the other biologists are saying is the next generation becomes a bunch of kissin' cousins."

"Oh-h-h." Meacham nodded. "So, what do we do? Fertility drugs, implant sheep, raise only women for the next generation." The president pointed a big hammy hand at the scientists, demanding an answer.

"Those things might help. Well, there are no sheep to implant, but fertility drugs can extend the normal reproductive age and a higher percentage of

134

the women in the next generation will help. Breeding grids can mathematically maximize genetic integrity. There is another remote possibility." Carl looked at the other scientists and sighed.

President Meacham's fist hit the table. "Spit it out, man. What is it?"

"There's an experimental prison in California—a federal sedation prison." Carl looked at the president. "It was in the news a while back."

"Heard of it. Hell, I supported it. The damn thing cost twice as much as the estimates. Damn Democrats raked me over the coals on that one." The president leaned forward. "What's it got to do with this?"

"According to the design plans, the prison has automated systems that include oxygen separators. If fuel reserves last, it's possible the inmates are still sedated and alive."

"So, we repopulate the planet with a bunch of criminals?"

"It's a long shot. We can't confirm how many females are housed there. Genetically, some might be undesirable, ahh . . . psychotic with a genetic component. However, if we can secure and implant cryogenic frozen embryos from any of dozens of fertility clinics?" Carl shrugged. "At this point, a womb is a womb."

* * * * *

The Seattle community divided up the work. An overseeing committee formed, but lacked authority beyond an outlet for the expression of the

communal will. Many of the survivors who lived
through the initial storm, "The Big Fart," suffered
with health issues and survived only because they
were on supplemental oxygen before the storm hit.
The able-bodied wearied of caring for them. Some
even called them "suckers," as they sucked up
precious oxygen and could not contribute to the
hard work of survival.

Mark and Jason took on the maintenance of the
generators and the oxygen separators. The
separators needed electricity to concentrate the life
sustaining oxygen—mission critical—so they
stockpiled spare parts and backups. Compressed
oxygen and air tanks became tertiary backups.

On the eighth day, Mrs. Larson, one of the
original survivors, recovered enough from her
surgery to monitor the shortwave from her
wheelchair. Jason and Emily stood in the corridor
when she rolled her wheelchair into the hall.

"Somebody, come quick. I got something on the
radio, a soldier. Hurry!"

Emily and Jason rushed into the tool shop. The
receiver hissed as usual but in between "We . . ."
Hiss. "United States . . ." *Hiss.* "Department of
Defense."

"Someone's out there!" Jason picked up the mic
and tuned into the same frequency. "Hello. This is
Sisters-of-Mercy Hospital in Seattle, Washington."

The transmission spiked and then became
clearer. "This is Sergeant McElroy, with the United
States Air Force in Colorado Springs. It's good to
hear from Seattle. To whom am I speaking? Over."

The Big Fart

Jason keyed his mic. "I'm Jason Adams. I'm here with fifty-one other survivors. We've had no other communication with anyone. How bad is the rest of the country?"

After a long hesitation the soldier cleared his throat. "I'll get my commanding officer. He can . . . ahh. Hold on."

Emily looked at Jason. "I didn't like the sound of that. It isn't just the West Coast, is it?" Others gathered around listening.

"Hello, Mr. Adams, this is General Burbage. Are the people there secure? How are you maintaining oxygen and life support?"

Jason glanced around. "We have . . . the hospital has its own generator and oxygen separator. Much of the upper building was destroyed, but we were able to seal the basement and keep it supplied with O_2."

"So, the life-support systems are stable?"

"Yes. What about the rest of the country?"

"The president and elements of the civilian government are here at the Cheyenne Mountain NORAD Complex."

"Did the storm sweep the entire country?"

"It covered the entire world. You are the largest civilian group of survivors we've contacted."

A collective moan issued from the gathering in the tool shop. Jason keyed the mic. "How many?"

"There is an atmospheric scientist here. He thinks the inversion will lift come summer, and that the atmosphere will remix and we'll be able to breathe again, if we can hang on for a few more weeks."

"Damn it. How many survivors?" Jason barked.

Silence. "Not enough. Your compound makes five hundred-twenty three within the United States. We have confirmation of another fourteen hundred or so throughout the world."

His worst fears confirmed, Jason's stomach knotted. Emily buried her head in her lap.

The receiver on the other end rustled. "Hello, I'm Gerald Sullivan, the president's chief of staff. How many able-bodies do you have?"

"Most of the survivors here at the hospital were patients." Jason wondered if he should list himself as able-bodied. "We have thirteen mostly healthy."

"I have to ask. How many females of reproductive age, between ages fifteen and fifty?"

Disconcerted, Jason scanned the room. People started counting on their fingers. "I don't know. Maybe . . . not many . . . five or six."

"I was afraid of that." Gerald continued, "Here, most of the military personnel are males. We are concerned with not only reproductive capacity, but with genetic diversity of the next generations."

Gerald spoke in the background, unintelligibly. Sullivan came back on.

"I have two staff members flying out to the West Coast. They will divert to Seattle and arrive tomorrow morning. I'd like you to clear any obstructions so they can land at Sea-Tac International Airport, and then provide them with ground transportation."

Mark, who stood behind Emily, stepped forward and yelled into the mic. "Hey! We're kinda busy trying to survive here. You can't order us around. We—"

The Big Fart

Screech! The receiver squelched. "By authority of the president under the Emergency Protocols Act, you are all under martial law. Any variance to orders will be dealt with harshly."

* * * * *

News of a dead world impacted older survivors the most. Silence hung like an egg-shell shroud, as if any comment, any attempt to divert attention, would break the fragile balance of sanity. At the cafeteria, Jason noted the young people, the under thirty, seemed to weather the news a little better. They exuded defiance, expressing existential angst through a variety of coping mechanisms. Anna dressed in goth and sassed her mother. The younger men hid behind a macho veneer and darkly glib humor.

What's blue and green, and dead all over? The whole frickin' planet.

Jason knew he should comfort people dealing with grief, but didn't know where to start. *Physician heal thyself.* He stayed busy as he hadn't come to terms with the new reality either.

Several women served breakfast from the kitchen counter. Jason took a plate and got in line behind Mark, who looked down at a pile of yellow protein on his plate. "What the fu—. Where's the eggs we brought in?"

An older woman shrunk back. "There were a couple rotten ones. We threw the whole batch out. All we have is powdered eggs."

"Threw them out!"

A Hope in Hell

"Can't you get more?" she responded.

"Get more from where? Those were the last eggs on the whole damn planet." Mark stalked off. "Ahh, shit!"

Jason leaned toward the woman. "Don't worry. He's got to adjust to the new reality." He walked over to a table where Emily and Valerie sat. Valerie, a middle-aged woman, had come over from the Virginia Mason Hospital. She recently underwent eye surgery, but could get around to help.

"Dr. Adams, you don't believe those awful people on the radio. I mean, how do they know? They can't have visited very many places, and not everyone knows how to set up a radio," Valerie begged.

Jason sat down. "We'll know more tomorrow. The presid—"

Valerie scowled. "It's the government's fault." Her voice grew more terse. "They should have seen this coming. Right? We survived. There must be thousands of small groups like us out there."

Valerie's voice went up an octave, tears emerged, and she covered her face.

Jason squeezed her shoulder. "I'm sure we'll keep finding more."

"My daughter, my grandchildren. They're in Florida. That general said it's the same all over the world."

Emily came around and hugged her. "Come on, hon. I'll walk you to your room."

They exited. Jason made a mental note to check on her later.

The Big Fart

That evening, he cleaned a crucial pressure regulator in the tool shop. The oxygen separators could not operate without the essential glass tube filled with mercury. Mark found a backup regulator, but only after searching most of the city. Jason carefully took the fittings apart and soaked them in a solvent.

"Hey, Mark. Why didn't you get more than one of these?"

Mark shook his head. "Would have loved to, amigo. Special order from Ohio. Damn lucky to have found one in—"

Bang! A gunshot echoed from the hall. They rushed to the corridor. Several people searched up and down wondering which direction the sound came from, until a woman screamed. A crowd formed in front of one of the side rooms. An older woman turned. "It's Arnold. He's shot himself."

Jason clenched his fists. "Is he . . ."

Someone nodded.

Shit! I failed.

An acquaintance offered, "He was eighty-two. I think he just didn't want to be a burden."

Mark took charge. "Everybody clear out. Ryan, you and I, morgue detail."

Jason returned to his room. The stress of the day weighed on his shoulders. He tried doing yoga to loosen his muscles, but the number eight rolled through his mind on an endless loop. *Eight billion people dead . . . eight billion . . . eight billion. Oh, shit! I better check on Valerie.* Jason slipped his shoes on and headed down the hall. Most of the women occupied the south section. *I think she's in #312.*

As he approached, Emily exited the room. "How is Val—"

Emily grimaced. She put her hand up and shook her head.

Jason started to enter the room. "What? No. She was . . . just a couple hours ago."

"Dr. Adams, she made a choice. Sleeping pills, I don't know how she got them. Not anyone's fault."

Jason pushed inside. Valerie lay in peaceful repose. He returned to the hall. Others gathered including Anna. Jason placed both hands on his head. "Shit. I was on my way."

"Man, two in one night," Anna quipped.

Emily scolded, "Anna. That's enough."

Anna stalked off.

Emily turned to the psychologist. "It's not anyone's fault."

Chapter XI

Forces of Nature

Jason couldn't sleep. His wrist imprint showed two in the morning. He took a photo card out of his wallet. *Eight billion, my sister, her family, all gone* . . . Pictures of family, growing up, high school, college, playing Hamlet on stage, graduation. Numbness came over him until he saw a 3D of his wife. Elaina. *Shadenfreude . . . her betrayal makes it easier.* He thought of the child he never had, and wept until his body shook. *Eight* . . . The weight of billions tightened his chest, vision and hearing became white noise—his chest heaved in uncontrolled grief.

Knock, knock. Jason gulped several breaths and looked up. A flashlight shone into the room.

"Shhh. That's not good for the others to hear." Emily's voice came from behind the light. She closed the door. She walked over and pointed to the picture card. "That can't be good. Put it away."

Between paroxysms Jason asked, "How do you grieve for eight billion people?"

Emily, the nurse, the practical one, opened a bottle of pills and took out two. "You don't think about it."

Jason gained control of his breath and stared at the bottle.

"Yeah, I only give out two at a time."

He hesitated.

"Well, what would your Carl Jung say, Mr. Psychologist?"

Jason didn't hesitate. "Find something more important than yourself."

"Work on that tomorrow, but right now, let's make it through the night."

Jason nodded, took the pills. Emily turned and walked to the door.

Something clicked, not in his mind, not on the conscious level, but something took over and drove him forward. If death caused this, could life redeem it? He simply rose and went to the door. Emily's hand rested on the door knob. He placed his hand on hers and pulled her back. She hesitated, then followed. They lay down. He reached for her, but she pushed him away.

"No. Go to sleep."

Jason turned over and lay on his side. She put an arm around him. He relaxed and slept.

Late the next morning, Jason awoke, and Emily was gone.

Two military men flew in from Cheyenne Mountain as promised. Everyone gathered in the basement cafeteria. Nearly a third came in wheelchairs; the able-bodied wheeled in a couple patients on gurneys. Colonel Jamison and Sergeant Davies faced the group from the front of the room. They wore crisp khakis and sat ramrod straight. They carried service forty-fives on their hips.

The five members of the recently formed community counsel sat in the front row. Jamison examined a stack of briefs on everyone in the compound.

Forces of Nature

Jason glanced at the papers as he walked to a seat in the front. *How in the hell did they get that so quickly?*

Jamison rapped his knuckles to quiet the room. "I'm Colonel Jamison and this is Sergeant Davies. I would like to thank Mark and Ryan for picking us up. We were sent here by direct order from the president of the United States. The colonel waved a hand over a 3D video card. President Meacham appeared, the hologram wobbled and then formed:

". . .experienced a level-four existential event— the existence of our species is threatened. We are doing everything within our powers to secure a future for the—" *Hiss.* ". . .emergency powers within the constitution, I am imposing martial law." The president stared directly at the camera. "You are all soldiers in the fight for survival of the human species. May God help us."

Colonel Jamison stopped the video. "Step one of our mission is to secure lives." He looked up. "As soldiers, you are all subject to executive orders."

A few collective moans scattered through the audience. Someone piped up. "You didn't bring a doctor. We need—"

The colonel held up his hand. "Please hold questions until the end. I'm very impressed with what has been accomplished here already. With fifty-two survivors, you are the largest civilian compound we've found."

Several people cleared their throats and someone spoke up. "There are about fifty, now."

Jamison furrowed his eyebrows.

After a moment of silence, Anna wisecracked, "That's a nice way to put it. This place is like a psych ward with razor blades."

That earned a harsh glare from Emily.

The colonel continued. "Life support systems are functional, and backups are accessible. I will work with able-bodied personnel to organize a preventative maintenance and supply program to insure air, water, and food."

Mark leaned over and whispered to Jason, "I thought that's what we've been doing."

"Step two of our mission is to find and secure as much of the human genome as possible." Jamison paused. "From what I understand, you have attempted just that. You've searched and put up light beacons. We are not likely to find more people through those methods. However, there is a federal experimental prison in Northern California. It's a sedation prison with automated life-support systems that may still be functioning. We have orders to investigate and secure its human gene pool."

"Are you talking about Hell's Gate Prison?" A lady in a wheelchair asked as the crowd reacted.

Mark protested, "What? They call it Hell's Gate for a reason—a bunch of mass murdering sickos."

The colonel shot back a steely glare and barked, "What's at stake is the survival of the human species." He lowered his voice. "Look at yourselves. Most of you are downhill of a boot top. Even with fertility drugs, the next generation will be half of this one. We need reproductive capacity. Scientists say a minimum of four hundred different mating pairs are needed or degeneracy and

146

inbreeding will be a problem. In other words, future generations will be a bunch of kissing cousins and have children with cognitive disorders, impaired immune systems, and a greater chance of retardation."

Again, a gray-haired woman in the crowd groused. "Are you are going to put murderers among us?"

Sergeant Davies replied, "Didn't Australia start this way?"

Jamison rapped his knuckles for quiet. "We will weigh reproductive potential against social detractors. And, we have an expert for that. Is Dr. Adams here?"

Jason didn't have to raise his hand, everyone turned to him.

"As our only psychologist, you are to determine which of the inmates might be redeemable."

"Colonel, how people react to psychoses-inhibiting drugs varies. I'm not qualified to—"

"I'm afraid you're all we've got!" Jamison erupted. "Females of reproductive age are a top priority."

Jason stole a glance at Emily.

"The mission is to stabilize the life-support systems and revive any useful assets. We need to send a squad to the prison ASAP. Sergeant Davies is in charge. The team shall consist of Emily Bloom, Mark Gunther, and Jason Adams. You depart tomorrow morning."

Colonel Jamison closed his folder and exited dismissively.

Jason sat back, stunned.

Mark shook his head. "When I got out of the army, I said I was never gonna follow another order. Damn gov'ment"

Emily turned to Jason, threw her hands up in a questioning gesture.

Early the next morning, Mark and Jason finished preparations. The maintenance man piled wrenches, pliers, and a hacksaw into his tool chest. "What would they do if I told that colonel to screw off?" He removed a pistol from a drawer.

Jason did a double take. "What?"

"It's for the serial killers. Some of them might need re-sedating." Mark put the gun in the top of the tool box. "We'll need an oxygen meter and a CO_2 meter from storage."

Jason marched down the hospital corridor to the storage room. Emily stood inside searching the shelves for supplies. Jason pulled the door closed behind him. "I want to thank you for last night."

Emily faced him. "We've all needed help sometime or other. Comforting people is part of the job." She crossed her arms. "But, that's that."

Jason's face turned ashen. "Sure. I didn't expect . . ."

"I have a daughter to raise. "You . . ." Emily grimaced. "You might not have that long. I'm sorry. Let's just focus on our assignment."

Jason grabbed an oxygen meter and turned to go, but paused. "She's okay."

"What?" Emily responded.

"Anna. The whole goth thing is a defense against how she feels." Jason kept his back to Emily. "Tell her . . . just tell her, if she wants to feel better, get over herself and help someone." Jason exited and returned to the shop.

Mark pointed to the oxygen bottles stacked by the door. "Get your gear on, sous chef, we'll load up the SUV."

Jason donned his portable gas-mask and helped Mark drag bottles and slide them into the back of vehicle. Looking up at the heavy gray cloud cover Jason shook his head. The odor of sulfur, rot, and ocean bottom brought up medieval images of hell.

"This is depressing."

"Yeah. Ain't exactly Palm Beach."

"I hope the scientists aren't just blowing smoke, that the atmosphere will remix and we'll be able to breathe again."

Mark snorted, "I think this trip's a waste of time if it don't." He pulled out a checklist. "Compressed oxygen, come-a-longs, cable, duct tape, acetylene torch. Everything I can think of. Got your anti-psycho pills, Freud?"

"Yep."

"Enough to calm a charging elephant?"

"Enough to tame a shrew."

"Let's find the asshole . . ." *Cough.* "I mean the sergeant and get this show on the road."

The team gathered at the end of the corridor with backpacks and breathing gear. Most of the residents came to say goodbye. The colonel repeated the mission objectives and offered motivation. "One of the scientists put it this way. Humans have only been around one hundred and forty thousand years, if we can't diversify the human gene pool, this will set us back a hundred millennia. God speed and good luck."

Emily reached to hug Anna. "I'll be back in a week."

Anna pulled away. "With a bunch of murderers and prostitutes. And, I was worried I'd get bored."

Emily snapped. "Look! I'm sorry you have to grow up so fast. But, if you want to feel better, get over yourself and help out." She picked up her gear and stalked toward the door.

Anna pouted, then ran and hugged her mom, hard. Emily looked surprised, but finally dropped her backpack and hugged her.

Anna sniffled. "I'm sorry."

Emily's gaze drifted to Jason with a quizzical thank you.

Chapter XII

Cerberus

The SUV proceeded down Interstate 5 swerving around abandoned vehicles, debris, and an occasional corpse. Nothing stirred, not even a bird in the sky. Sergeant Terrance Davies veered around a vehicle and slammed the brakes.

"Your turn, Adams."

Jason adjusted his respirator, got out, and looked inside a blocking sedan. *Damn, a corpse inside.* Jason opened the door and reached for the man slumped over the steering wheel. His grip punctured the skin on the corpse's arm. *Shit!* The stench even leaked through his half-mask. His stomach curled and he immediately retched. He yanked off the respirator too late. Puke swathed the inside. Jason pulled the mask off, and tried to cover his nose as he continued retching.

Mark tapped his shoulder and handed him water and a towel. The handyman pushed the dead man over, reached inside, and tried to start the car. Nothing. He marched back to the SUV.

Jason recovered by the time Mark pulled the winch cable out. The psychologist took the end, crawled under the sedan and hooked it to the frame.

Sergeant Davies winched the vehicle aside. Jason unhooked the sedan, wound the cable, and then climbed back in.

Emily handed him a tissue and a stick of gum. "Do you feel alright? Any shortness of breath? Taking your beta blockers?"

Jason nodded.

They stopped for the night near Roseburg, Oregon. Using a camp stove, they boiled water for freeze-dried dinners. The four travelers slept sitting half upright in the SUV.

They crossed into California the next afternoon. A partly overturned trailer blocked the freeway. The van lay against a guardrail with the tractor still attached and its rear wheels in the air. Sergeant Davies slowed to a stop.

Mark nodded at the overturned semi. "If I can loosen the coupler, we can move the cab and get around it."

Davies looked at his map and pointed to the exit ramp. "No need. This is it."

He swerved around the tractor to pull off the freeway. He followed a frontage road and steered onto a lengthy driveway, where he stopped in front of a heavy steel sliding gate. The dim sunset cast dimmer shadows across the entrance to Hell's Gate Prison. An ornate, but formidable, fence surrounded the site. "Here we are, ladies and gentlemen. Step one, find the prison."

"Prison, you mean the gates of hell." Mark nodded to the fallen sign covered with downed branches. The foliage left only the word *"Hell"* visible.

They donned respirators, checked their tanks, and exited the vehicle. Mark examined the gate. "Jason, get the acetylene torch out of the back."

Cerberus

Jason wandered down the fence line to a fallen tree lying athwart the wrought iron pickets. "Hey, no razor-wire. I think we can climb over."

Jason started up at the base of the twenty-inch-diameter pine. As he neared the fence, the tree narrowed. What looked easy for a ten-year-old was a challenge for a forty-something with an iffy heart. Sitting on the trunk, he threw one leg over the pickets. Scooting forward, the jeans on his other leg caught on the jagged metal.

"Ahh!" He slipped sideways, threw his arms around the trunk and hung precariously with his pants caught on the spiked pickets.

Emily gasped. "Jason!"

Sergeant Davies stood there nonplussed. "Idiot. The last thing we need is casualties."

Mark ran over. "Hold on. I gotcha." He shinnied up the trunk, took a pair of tin snips from his tool belt and cut the psychologist free. Mark gave him a hand as Jason pushed through branches 'til he cleared the fence pickets. He clung to one branch and awkwardly swung down to the ground.

Mark followed. "Careful there, Peter Pan."

Mark and Jason proceeded to the gate house. Glass shards from its broken windows covered the interior.

Mark swept the shards from a control console, flipped a switch, and a diode lit up. "We got power!" He pressed several buttons. A lock clicked and a motor whirred, drawing the gate open.

"Wahoo!"

They climbed back into the vehicle and pulled up to the building. The sergeant scanned his notes.

"It doesn't look that big," Jason observed.

"Most of it is underground. Everybody check their bottles and get your headlamps. Mark, get your tools." The sergeant checked his forty-five. "Let's see if anybody's alive."

Davies kicked debris from the front doors. He cupped two hands against the glass and peered inside. "Nothing." He tried the handle. "Locked."

Mark set his tool box down and took out a steel bar and hammer. "Shouldn't be too hard. Prisons are made to keep people in, not out." Forcing the bar into the seam, he swung the hammer down. *Bam!* The doors opened, and the four survivors entered the darkened foyer.

Sergeant Davies and Mark examined the reception-area guard station. The military officer tried a light switch. "I thought the generators were running?"

Mark shrugged. "Donno. Maybe a breaker tripped."

Emily and Jason wandered into a dark side room. Murky shapes lay on the floor. They turned on their headlamps. Jason flinched—dead guards, mouths agape in silent screams. He got a whiff of decay through the respirator.

"Same here as in Seattle. They all died gasping for air."

Sergeant Davies and Mark walked a corridor and found more dead uniformed guards. A plaque with a picture of "Warden Jeff Ramsey" hung on the door. Davies peeked inside. He pointed to a couple of computer monitors. "The records should be here."

154

Cerberus

They met back in the foyer. "Looks like all the guards are dead." The sergeant examined his notes. "The mechanical room is on the next floor down." Their headlamps swept the area until Emily found a stairwell.

"Abandon all Hope" hung above the doors.

Mark tapped his oxygen bottle. "About an hour and a half left."

"Let's get to it." The sergeant led the way through open steel bars that guarded the stairs. They descended, light beams stabbing the darkness. The second-floor landing held an alcove with a desk, and another set of closed steel bars. Their squad leader pulled on them, to no avail.

Mark examined the lock. "It's got power, but we need a pass code." He put his fingers around the bars and held them up in measurement. "An inch of hardened steel. Damn, it'll take half a day to cut through that."

As he started back up the stairs, Jason stepped forward.

"Let me try." Jason punched the key box, "Hellsgate." Nothing. "Hades." Nothing.

Sergeant Davies piped up. "Quit wasting time. Adams, help Mark get the torch.

"Dante." Nothing. "Cerberus."

"What are you going to do, say open sesa—"

Pssst. The gate slid open.

Davies's jaw dropped.

Jason shrugged. "People like to use mythical references for passwords."

Mark turned. "Psych-man, you might be useful after all."

The sergeant looked at the keypad readout. "Cer . . .ber . . . us?"

"Cerberus, the three-headed dog that guarded the . . ." Jason motioned toward the corridor, "underworld."

The only light on the second floor came from a faint eerie glow at the far end of a long hall. They preceded, Jason's breath quickened, and his headlamp darted side to side.

Mark looked back at the psychologist. "Stop it man. You're making me nervous."

Emily's headlamp focused on a side room door. "Hadn't we better check to see if anyone's alive?"

Their leader nodded, stepped over, and pulled his sidearm.

Jason frowned. "What are you expecting?"

Mark set his tool box down and took out the pistol. "Serial fucking killers, that's what I'm expecting."

The sergeant opened the door, stepping aside for Mark.

"Oh, that's brave, Davies," Mark snapped.

The officer snorted. "Shut up. I'm the squad leader."

Emily strode forward. "Oh, for Christ's sake." She started to enter the inky blackness, but Jason put out an arm to intervene. Taking his headlamp off, he held it high to light up more area—like a crucifix against evil.

Jason walked between two rows of pods. Emily and Mark followed close behind.

Emily examined a control panel on one of the pods. "It's working. The system's still working. They're alive."

The controls displayed: *"TEMP. 88; PULSE RATE 45 BEATS A MINUTE."*

"Bless those Detroit diesels." Mark rubbed the dust from a sarcophagus viewing plate. Inside lay a ghostly pale man with long white hair. "Ugly."

Sergeant Davies wiped the name plate from a couple pods. "Eric Watsjold? Ahh. . . Lee Johnson? Where are the women?"

Jason shrugged. "We need to look at the records."

"Enough, let's get to the generators." Their leader pointed back to the hall.

They marched down to the far end of the corridor with their footsteps eerily echoing back from behind them.

Mark labored, lugging his toolbox. "Shit, this is longer than a Costco aisle."

Standard overhead lights illuminated the mechanical room.

Sergeant Davies turned to the maintenance man. "Why are the lights on here but not elsewhere?"

"Man, I don't know. Maybe it's programmed in. After fuel gets low, it shuts down nonessential loads."

Jason stepped around the control console. He jumped back, startling the others.

Mark strode forward, pistol raised, stopped and stared at the lone figure sitting at the desk. "Shit. You scared me. He's dead?" The maintenance man hesitantly reached over and tapped the corpse with his pistol. Mark exhaled and lowered the gun. "He's dead." The maintenance man spun him around.

"Hey, is that the warden guy? What's-his-name?" Davies leaned closer. "Jeff something." He pointed to the tubing thirty feet away. "He tried to . . ." The sergeant followed the tube to the oxygen generator. "He tapped the O_2 system. Why did he die?"

Jason stepped behind the chair and pushed him well out of the way to the aisle between the generators. Returning to the console he punched the keyboard. The monitor woke up, showing the carbon dioxide levels in the inmates. "The inmate readouts are here. They are all alive. The last thing Mr. Warden did was crank up the oxygen flow. That's why they've survived!"

Mark looked back at the man in the chair. "Now, that's dedication."

Jason typed some more. Schematics of the fuel tanks showed up. "Mark, what does this mean?"

"Damn. We're down to five gallons. Holy shit! We gotta be burning five or six gallons an hour, even at low usage." Mark shook his head. "It's goodbye sleepy-town."

The sergeant peered over Jason's shoulder. "We made it just in time. Mark, how long to get some fuel down here?"

"Get a tanker? Forever." The maintenance man threw his hands in the air. "Four, five, hours at least. There's less than an hour of fuel left. It's tits up for Murderers' Row."

Wham! Sergeant Davies slammed the console. "Shit! God damn it." He stomped around in a circle and spat, "The colonel will have my ass." His head snapped up. "Emily, Jason, what can we do? We can save fuel. How?"

Mark piped in, "We could cut off half of them and lower the load. The generators will use less fuel, but that'll buy us only another half-hour. Not enough."

Jason sat lost in thought.

Emily jumped up. "We can find the women. Use our compressed air bottles to oxygenate a room and save as many lives as we can."

"Yeah. Emily's plan. Let's move. Start searching the pods for women. Emily and Jason take this floor. Mark and I will get the bottles." Davies marched out with Mark and Emily behind.

"Wait!" Jason raised his head. "There was a diesel rig out on the highway."

Mark stopped in his tracks so suddenly Emily bumped into him. The sergeant, halfway out of the mechanical room, turned back impatiently. "Hey, come on. Move it!"

Mark jabbed his thumb toward Jason. "Psych-man's right. Diesel rigs have big tanks. They'll hold about two-hundred gallons."

Davies challenged, "How do we know it's not empty."

"A good driver never runs on empty."

"Can we get it down here in time?" Jason looked back at the computer screen. "Shit, it's dropped to under five gallons.

The sergeant barked orders, "Mark, you and I will get the rig. Jason, Emily shut down any unnecessary electrical loads. Let's go, go, go!"

* * * * *

Mark jumped into the SUV as Sergeant Davies started the vehicle and turned on the headlights.

They raced out of the parking lot, sped along the winding, redwood-lined drive, and up the freeway exit ramp. They stopped by the overturned diesel rig they saw earlier.

Mark donned his respirator, jumped out, and examined the tractor illuminated in the SUV's headlights. The trailer coupler held the rear wheels off the ground. He opened the cab's gas tank and poked in a stick. It came out coated with diesel.

"Almost full. Over two hundred gallons here." He gave Davies a thumbs-up. "Help me unhitch the trailer."

Mark took out a hammer and banged on the trailer lock lever. Nothing. Mark banged harder. He rummaged around, found a four-foot bar and plied it as a lever. "Damn it."

At the same time, Sergeant Davies climbed on top of the tractor bed and jumped up and down. It didn't budge.

"We're running out of time!" Davies shouted.

"Get the winch, Sergeant." Terrance pulled the cable from the front of the SUV. Mark wrapped it around the coupler. Terrance got in and retracted the cable, the SUV's tires screeched and inched forward, but the coupler didn't budge. Mark hammered again. Nothing.

Chapter XIII

Don't Wake the Dragon

Jason searched electrical energy schematics on the computer as Emily watched over his shoulder. The psychologist shook his head. "Everything is already shut down except life support."

"Not this." Emily flipped off the mech-room lights and turned her headlamp on.

"You scared me." Jason switched to his headlamp. "There's a room labeled Life-Support on the first floor. Let's check that out. Maybe something there can be shut down."

"We can look at some of the pod rooms, too. If there are empty pods, we can turn them off."

Jason and Emily exited the mechanical room. Their lights barely reached the far end of the corridor and the stairwell. Their footsteps echoed back in an eerie reverberation. Jason listened nervously. *Now, that's creepy.*

Emily started to jog, but looked back, clearly realizing Jason couldn't keep up.

"Go ahead. I'll follow as best as I can," Jason offered.

"That's okay. You're doing fine.

He felt relieved upon reaching the end of the corridor. They ascended the stairs and entered the foyer. Now, completely dark outside, their light beams found two corridors at the far end of the lobby. "Infirmary" marked one door. The other loomed unmarked.

They skipped the infirmary and entered the next door and into a hallway, passing offices and a small commercial kitchen. *"Sedation and Life Support Systems"* marked a set of double doors at the end. One side stood ajar. Red warning signs on the panels read, *"Authorized Personnel Only."* Jason pushed on the door, but something blocked it. He pushed harder and it moved. Though accustomed to the unsavory odors that occasionally leaked through the face-seals on his respirator, Jason still couldn't handle the wave of strong putrescence from beyond the door. Jason gagged, stepped back, and put his hands on his knees.

Emily almost smirked. "Yeah. The body fluids of life and death." She stepped inside shining her light on a dead guard lying just inside. "You should work the detox unit sometime."

She swept her light around the chamber—large vats of chemicals fed plenum reservoirs that fed chemical pumps that, in turn, fed a network of pipes and tubing.

Jason entered, careful to not look down at the guard. Motors softly whirred and liquids burbled throughout the maze. "This is what keeps them nourished and sedated. We don't want to mess with this." His light caught a large cylindrical tank in the center of the room. The label read *"Ventilation Mixture."*

"Hey, this is what they breathe." He tapped the cylinder. 'It's pressurized. So, if the generator quits, this could last a little longer and keep them breathing."

"Good. Let's hope we don't need to test that theory."

They exited and returned to the lobby. Emily stuck her head inside the infirmary and turned off her lamp. Seeing a lot of diodes and a couple lights on, she entered. Small lights illuminated two holding cells.

Jason swung his beam onto a dark shape on the floor of one of the cells, which illuminated an orange-clad figure. "We can turn that light off. He doesn't need it anymore."

Emily tried the cell door, but it was locked.

"All that dark humor is starting to rub off on you."

Jason found a broom, extended it inside the cell and, after a few tries, flicked off the light switch. The nurse went into a side room that held several large machines.

"My gosh, this place is well equipped—an MRI, even an operating room. The MRI is in standby mode. We don't need that." She switched it off. In another room, she unplugged a culture incubator. "Pretty small potatoes as far as electrical load is concerned. Let's check out the pod rooms."

They descended the stairwell, returning to subfloor two. Jason entered the first pod room. The hairs on his neck stood at attention as he walked between the racks of sarcophagi. He shined his light on one of the pod viewing-windows. "Empty here."

Emily started at the other end. "These are empty, too." She stepped to the next set. "I think they're all empty."

"We better check each one."

Emily looked in the last pod. "Nobody home. Now, how do we turn them off?"

"Over here." Jason found a master control panel on the wall. Holding two buttons at the same time, all the diode lights on the sarcophagi went dark. "Next."

They did the same in the first five rooms that lay empty. They hustled out into the corridor and Jason checked the time. "It's been forty-five minutes. Where the hell are Mark and Davies?" Jason glanced back up the hall. "Hopefully we bought a little more time."

They found the sixth room half occupied. Jason looked at the control unit on the wall. "We can't turn off individual pods from here. He walked over and examined the controls on an empty sarcophagus. "There's a deep sleep mode and a revive mode and . . . yeah, here it is." The pod controls blinked and shut down.

Emily hustled to the next pod to turn it off. "How did you do that? Push the operational menu and then—"

Hummm. Silence.

It took several seconds for the full meaning of the silence to dawn on Jason. The soft vibration that kept the inmates sedated and alive had shut down.

"Damn!" Jason marched toward the door. He heard a click. He panicked and lunged for the door lever—locked.

Emily ran over and tried. "It wasn't locked before."

Jason looked about nervously. "It must default to lock down if the power fails. Shit!" Jason thumped the door with his fist. "Solid. It's made to keep people in. We won't get out without power tools." He looked nervously down the row of pods. "We're screwed."

* * * * *

Sergeant Davies put the SUV in reverse and tried again. Tires squealed with no result.

Mark marched back to the vehicle. "Get out. Let me in. Hurry." He slid behind the wheel and pulled forward, giving the cable slack. "Stand back!" He jammed the SUV into reverse, violently jerking the cable taut and rocking the tractor.

The sergeant backed farther out of the way.

Mark did it again with a screech of metal and the cable snapped. *Bang!* The broken end flew back and struck the vehicle, but the cab teetered and . . . *Whoomph.* It came loose from the coupler.

"Yeah, baby!" Mark pumped his fist.

"Wah-hoo! Alright, let's get this puppy down there."

Mark ran to the cab and opened the door. A corpse lay across the front seat. "Ahh, sunova bitch."

He grabbed an arm to yank it out of the cab, but thought better of it once he felt the soft mushy flesh. Tightening the straps on his respirator, he climbed up and pushed the body over far enough so he could sit behind the wheel. The engine cranked and started. Gears ground as Mark rolled the cab to the exit ramp and sped toward the prison. Davies followed in the SUV.

The truck's headlights revealed a number of standpipes dotting the gravel pad on the south side of the building. Mark steered to the middle of them and stomped the brakes. He jumped out and examined them.

"This one's the fuel tank." As the soldier bounced out of the SUV, Mark put his ear to an exhaust stack. "Sergeant. I don't hear the generator running."

Davies panicked. "Oh crap!"

Mark pulled the cab closer. He exited, found a hose from his tool box, and put one end into the cab's diesel tank. He tried to take the cap off the three-inch steel pipe, but it was locked.

* * * * *

Jason sat on one of the racks for the pod units.

Emily walked over and peered apprehensively inside a pod window. "Stable so far. The gas tank you saw must still be supplying air, for now." She sat down across from him. "When I was a little girl my dad played a game with me called Don't Wake the Dragon. He put one of my toys beside him and pretended he was asleep. I'd try to steal my toy back without waking him. Of course, he always woke up and grabbed me, and I screamed and giggled." Emily smiled.

"You must have had a good relationship with your father."

"Oh, yeah. We—"

Thump.

"What was that?" Emily shined her light deep into the racks of sarcophagi.

Thump.

She spun around. The second noise came from the opposite direction.

"Uh oh. They're waking up!" Jason stood and hesitantly shined his lamp into the window of the pod he stood next to. The inmate's eyelids twitched. "Damn. This one's emerging from deep sedation into REM sleep. He's dreaming. He'll be awake in a few minutes."

"Jason. What'll we do?" Emily's light beam darted up and down the rows. "Shall we hide?"

Whump.

Emily swung her light to the psychologist's face. "Can they open their pods from the inside? They can't just remove their tubes, can they?"

"I don't know." Jason tried the lid he stood next to. It lifted easily. "Unfortunately, yes."

Thump. Thump.

"Turn the lights out, move over here as far from the pods as we can. Their tubes won't—" *Bam!* "Reach."

They turned their headlamps off and hid behind an empty sarcophagi. The psychologist held one index finger against his lips to indicate silence.

A scuffing sound came from the pods. *Thump. Bam!*

Jason strained his eyes. In the thick darkness, he wouldn't have seen an up-close barn door. *Look at the diodes, anything move in front of them?*

Scuffle. Thump.

A Hope in Hell

Did I hear a pod open? Jason cupped a hand over his ear.

Wham!

* * * * *

Mark swung his hammer at the locked fuel cap and broke it off. He stuck a hose into the truck's fuel tank and sucked on the other end to start a siphon. Spitting the diesel out of his mouth with a grimace, the maintenance man slipped the flowing hose into the fueling pipe. After a minute he gave a thumbs-up.

"Okay, they can restart it." He banged on the piping to signal that it was refueled. "Start the effin' generator, you idiots." Mark waited for a while, then stood up. "Sergeant, hold the hose. I'm going down there."

As soon as the SUV screeched to a halt outside the main entrance, Mark bailed out and ran to the stairwell. Turning his light on, he pounded down the steps. The long second-floor corridor extended for what seemed like forever. *Where the hell is everyone?* He ran halfway along the hall before shouting, "Jason! Emily! Hey, start the generator!"

* * * * *

Emily heard Mark and let out a stifled, "Here—" She stopped, so as not to compromise their hiding spot.

Thump. Scuffle.

"What the hell?" Jason turned his lamp on shining it down the row of pods. All the lids remained closed. He ran to the door and hammered on it. *Whap, whap, whap.*

"Mark! Terrance! We're in here. Mark!"

Emily came up behind him, but shined her light in the direction of the pods.

Thump.

Jason turned his lamp to highlight more of the sarcophagi, but still pounded the door. *Whap, whap.*

Whump. One of the lids partially opened. Emily screamed. "Eeeek! Jason."

Whap, whap. "Mark!"

Burrooom. Hummm.

"The generator! It's started." Jason tried the door again. "Still locked."

Wham! One of the pod lids flew open. Jason hustled over to it and reached up to close the lid— an orange clad arm emerged. Emily scurried up behind him.

Cough, cough. The inmate's eyes opened.

Jason managed to stuff the arm in and slam the lid. "Emily, sit on this."

Wham! Another pod behind him flew open.

Unmindful of his heart condition, he hustled over to it. An arm shot up and grabbed him around the throat. Jason struggled against it.

"Eeeek!" Emily rushed over and pried at the choking fingers.

The inmate sat up, stared at Jason, and looked down at the IV in his arm. His head nodded, his hand slipped from Jason's throat and he reached for the IV. His eyelids closed and he slumped back into the sarcophagus.

The door opened, a light shone on them. "What the hell you guys doing in here? Playing grab-ass?" Mark's voice sounded reassuring, despite the sarcasm.

Jason rubbed his bruised neck. "Just getting to know the prisoners. Some of them have a few issues."

Emily crossed her arms. "We were locked in, Mark, and if I wasn't so glad to see you, I'd call you a real jerk.

After checking a dozen rooms to make sure the inmates remained sedated, they met in the mechanical room.

Sergeant Davies nodded at the computer. "So, how much time do we have now?"

Jason turned on the power and brought up the fuel schematic. "Looks like thirty-some hours at this rate."

"How do we re-oxygenate the whole building?" The sergeant turned to Mark.

"What? That will burn twice as much fuel!"

Emily added, "We'll be working inside for days. The women we revive may not be that stable. They'll need a breathable environment. Not to mention, I gotta get out of this mask."

Jason touched his chest. "I agree, this is hard on the system."

"Crap," Mark groused.

Davies stood up "Let's get to it. Seal the external vents. Mark, how do we install the CO_2 scrubbers and reroute the oxygen separators?"

Mark stepped around to the oxygen consoles, examined the venting, and muttered, "Mark, do this, Mark do that. I'm joining a damn union, man."

Don't Wake the Dragon

* * * * *

By two in the morning, Jason slumped with exhaustion. They had finished rerouting some of the ductwork feeding the two oxygen separators, and reset them to maximum output. They plodded upstairs like zombies.

Terrance tapped his mask. "How long 'til we're breathable?"

Jason waved the meter around the lobby, shaking his head. "Seventeen parts per million oxygen, carbon dioxide still nearly ten. Several hours."

Davies announced, "We'll sleep in the SUV again."

"Lovely." Mark looked at Jason and Emily's duct tape job around the outside doors. "Hey, duct tape isn't going to make it. There's some rubber stripping in the back of the SUV."

Jason nodded. "Tomorrow."

They exited the building, temporarily resealed the doors, and tossed empty portable oxygen cylinders into a growing pile outside. Stumbling into the SUV, they removed their masks. Too tired to talk, Emily passed out sandwiches. Jason took two bites and fell asleep.

* * * * *

He awoke to the rustlings of movement. The other three, already awake, shuffled through their gear in the overcrowded vehicle.

Sergeant Davies yawned and stretched. He looked back at the psychologist. "Let's go, soldier."

Emily turned in her seat. "How are you doing?"

"I don't have much stamina."

"Make sure you take your blood thinner."

She passed Jason some kind of fortified liquid. He drank and stared out at the perpetual gloom of the post-apocalyptic cloud cover.

As they reentered the building, Jason waved the oxygen meter sensor through the air. He gave a thumbs-up. "Twenty-four percent, damn near perfect." He removed his mask and immediately regretted it.

Mark winced in pain. "Holy gofer guts. Smells bad."

Davies pulled his respirator back, took one whiff and replaced it. "Yeah, DT. Psych Man, you and me."

Emily looked at the sergeant. "Sergeant Davies, what's DT?"

"Dignified transfer. Better known as mortuary services. Em, can you go with Mark to find a fuel tanker?"

She held out one hand and then the other. "Umm. Morgue detail or a scenic drive. Gladly. And, another thing. I'm tired of calling you sergeant. May I call you Terrance?"

"Sure."

Mark jumped in. "Ahh, I was just getting used to Sergeant Butthead."

Outside the building, the two men slid a corpse off of a gurney and laid it in a row with five other bodies all dressed in guard uniforms. Jason surveyed the bodies.

"I suppose we should bury them."

"No scavengers. No hurry. Eventually we'll get a backhoe and do a mass burial."

They both turned their heads to the sound of an approaching vehicle. Terrance watched as a stainless-steel tanker rounded the corner. "That was fast."

From the cab, Mark gave the horn a couple blasts as he drove to the south side of the building. Emily pulled up in the SUV and stepped out.

"We found a tanker on the freeway only twelve miles down the road. Mark said it had about four thousand gallons."

Terrance jumped in the vehicle. "Yay, about time we got a break. Let's go help him."

Jason, fatigued from dragging corpses around, grudgingly climbed in. Emily drove to the south side and they helped Mark fill the diesel tanks. Terrance nodded toward the building. "Let's go see how much we've got."

They entered the building, descended the stairwell, and started the long walk to the mechanical room. Emily stopped, crossing her arms she looked back.

"Terrance, the last door locked us in with a bunch of murderers. I know I'm being paranoid, but just to be sure, let's block open the steel door to the stairwell."

"Good idea. Mark, do it."

"That door didn't lock last time."

"What if somebody came and . . ." Emily stopped, realizing irrationality of her fear.

"Hell, no. You don't get it. There's nobody alive here. Nobody else on the whole planet." Regardless of the protest, Mark stomped back to the entrance. "No way, no how." He pulled the station desk across the threshold, its metal feet screeching on the concrete.

Jason turned on the mech-room lights and its computer. Calling up the fuel graph, the gauge showed more than four-thousand gallons. Mark asked for the consumption graph, and Jason changed screens. "About eight gallons an hour. Twenty days at this rate."

Jason logged into the personnel records. "We should see if what we came for is here."

The maintenance man chimed in, "You mean pussy?"

Emily narrowed her eyes. "Jesus, this is serious guys. Criminals or not, they're human beings."

Everyone looked onscreen as Jason scrolled through files. "Inmate records, rap sheets, psychiatric profiles, medical records, and—I'll be damned—an entire floor of female prisoners."

Sergeant Davies pointed to the screen. "Bingo! Let's get moving."

The psychologist held up a hand. "Oh, no, I have to screen them first. Check their psych profiles. It'll take some time."

Mark scowled. "What? How long's that gonna take?"

The sergeant exhaled in disappointment. "He's right. This'll take a couple days."

Jason continued searching the records. Emily tapped his shoulder. "Let's check the infirmary for medical supplies, antidepressants, psych drugs."

"Wait. I have to see . . ."

Emily looked over the psychologist's shoulder. "See what?"

"One chance in two-thousand, the medical records have . . ." Jason typed in his blood type, RH factor, and serotype, and hit the search key. He sat back and sighed. "Exactly one."

Mark looked at the screen. "I know of that guy. The serial killing priest, righteous bad."

Davies chimed in. "Holy shit! Reverend William Branson—human sacrifices and all that."

Emily leaned in. "He's your heart donor match?"

Everyone looked at the psychologist.

Jason nodded. "I was just curious. I know there's no hospitals, no heart surgeons."

Emily looked at Terrance. "What about in Colorado?"

"Negative. The colonel has Dr. Adam's profile. He checked already. There were a couple doctors, but no heart surgeons." Sergeant Davis spoke as if he were delivering a weather report.

"The ethics of taking a sedated person's heart. Not exactly Hippocratic," Jason puzzled.

Mark scoffed, "Oh, hell. The guy's a serial killer. Screw him."

"Let's get moving. We can check him out on the way. Maybe a surgeon will still pop up somewhere sometime." Davies led them back along the corridor.

The four stopped at pod room number seven.

"He's in here." Jason indicated.

Mark dropped his toolbox and, again, took out his pistol.

Emily mocked him. "Why? Mr. Nobody-else-on–the-whole-planet."

Terrance pulled his side arm, too. "We had an interruption of the sedation system. I know the computer indicated everyone is still asleep, but better safe than sorry."

Jason led the way, his lamp illuminating the rows of sarcophagi. Walking between rows, he hit his head on an overhead support. "Ouch!" The blow knocked him to the ground and sent his headlamp skittering across the floor.

Emily jumped, letting out a guttural scream. She backed into Mark, knocking the gun from his hand.

Bang! The pistol hit the floor and discharged.

Terrance Davies aimed his sidearm and waved his light to-and-fro. "Adams, report. What's going on? Adams!"

Jason recovered. "Nothing. I hit my head. I fell. I'm fine."

Davies lowered his weapon. "Damn it. You could'a killed somebody. Mark, never take your safety off again."

"Screw you, butthead. Tell this sucker to watch it." Mark scooped up his pistol and checked it.

"Stop it, you two. Let's find this guy." Emily stooped, picked up the errant light, and examined a bump on Jason's head. "You'll live." She began searching the names on the pods. "Did he have a pod number?"

"Ahh . . . I don't remember. Only twenty-four pods. We can find him." Jason rubbed the dust from a readout.

Terrance moved between the rows. "Hey. I know this guy."

"You find your daddy?" Mark quipped.

"Bob Bragga. He went crazy and killed a bunch of Yankee fans with a baseball bat." The military man peered inside the sarcophagus.

"Can't say I blame him." Mark continued searching.

"Anybody remember a Hans Fleischer?" Emily looked inside. "Fat and bald."

"Nope."

"I've heard of him from somewhere, can't recall." Emily scratched her forehead.

"Here he is. William Branson." Mark gazed inside. "Ugly. Was he a religious wacko or something?"

Jason stepped over to examine the readouts on the serial killer's sarcophagi. "The religious angle was probably just an outgrowth of a dissociative disorder. I'm guessing he had a grandiose sense of self, superficial charm, and lack of remorse." The psychologist peered inside. "Everything looks normal."

"Alright we know he's here, and he is one effed up dude. It's lunchtime, boys and girls." Mark stomped out.

They exited, leaving pod room seven with only the glow of red diodes and green-hued digital readouts.

A Hope in Hell

* * * * *

Within the darkness of pod room seven, sparks flew, leaving burn marks on a circuit board as smoke curled out from a bullet hole in the wall control panel. The sarcophagi controls failed to default mode: Revive.

The body temperatures of the occupants slowly increased. The readouts moved upward to 88.3°. . . *Flicker*. . . 88.4. . . 88.6.

The heart rates moved toward normal. *Tha-thump. Tha-thump. Tha-thump* . . . *47*. . .*48* beats a minute. Inside the sarcophagi, eyes twitched and muscles jerked as inmates rose out of deep sleep. Hours passed.

Reverend Branson's eyes twitched under closed eyelids. His eyes sprung open, his pulse rate climbed. *Tha-thump. Tha-thump. Tha-thump*. From 90, to 120, 130, and 140.

Bang. The lid of the sarcophagus flew clear. Pale, alert, he sat up. Prison orange tunic soaked in sweat—he ripped out the IVs, lifted himself over the side of the pod, and fell to the floor.

Reverend Branson staggered to the door on wobbly legs, cracked it open, and peered down the corridor. His bare feet padded on the concrete as he tottered toward the mechanical room. He found the dead warden perched in a chair between the generators. His gnarled hands patted the warden's pockets, reached in, and emerged with a multi-tool knife.

Chapter XIV

Road Trip

The C-21A, a military version of a small Lear jet, bounced and shuddered as it rose through the thick cloud cover dubbed the Devil's Inversion. It broke through into sunshine at twenty-two thousand feet and a wave of euphoria washed over its three passengers. Bill blinked and peered out the sunlit portal. He felt Neolithic, like he wanted to raise his arms, bathe in the dancing yellow photons, and sing praises to an ancient God.

It's still here. We can get our Earth back. He turned to the other two scientists, wondering if this had the same effect on the Frenchman Jean Girard and the biologist Carl Waisanen.

Bill put his face back to the portal's brilliance as Apollo raced his chariot across the sky. *Gerald Sullivan must have recognized the importance of the satellite information.* He had sold the president on this mission with the duel goals of reestablishing communication with the weather satellites and retrieving frozen human embryos from a fertility clinic in Miami. *He did alright.*

The atmospheric scientist closed his eyes and turned directly to the sun, sensing the yellow orb through closed eyelids. He then looked down at the thick dark layer of clouds with an ominous reverie. *Eight billion people dead, warming Earth, millions of species extinct. . . we may be next.*

A Hope in Hell

The pilot announced their approach to Cape Canaveral and Kennedy Space Center. The C-21A descended through the inversion layer and broke out above an umbral bay. He circled the tarmac— though the expansive tarmac offered ample landing area, the pilot searched to find a path clear of debris. The pilot must have decided on an approach. He circled again, dropped quickly, and bounced to a sudden halt.

On the ground, the pilot and two of the scientists unloaded several carts of supplemental oxygen bottles and supplies, while Bill searched the airport for a vehicle. He found an ambulance and drove it up to the aircraft.

The pilot set a box on top of the stack. "I checked out your shortwave radio. Couldn't contact Colorado. You'll have to set up an antenna, but if we lose contact, I'll be back in five days." He looked at the inventory. "Got enough oxygen?"

Girard shook his head. "No. Only two days' worth. We have to find more supplies."

Bill assured him, "The airport's emergency gear will have scuba tanks and rebreathers."

"Be careful." The pilot climbed back aboard. "Good luck. And, stand back."

The jet engine came to life with a high-pitched whine, the plane taxied down the tarmac, lifted off, and disappeared back into the thick inversion layer.

They loaded the supplies, sealed up the vehicle's vents, installed CO_2 filters, and turned on an oxygen bottle. Bill pulled off his respirator. "Glad to get out of this thing."

Waisanen sat in the back seat, checking the number of bottles. "When I trained for biohazards we never wore them for more than thirty minutes at a time. It's a strain on the heart."

"That's why we have to know if this will reverse itself." Bill steered toward the main terminal. "If people know they just have to hang on 'til summer . . ."

The biologist changed his tone. "Sure, but the first priority is to secure the embryos."

"*Ecoutez*, satellite repair must come first." Girard looked to Bill.

"Carl, there may be systems that are not meant to be shut down. We could lose communication with the very satellites that might save us. We need that information. Cape Canaveral first."

"If the damn atmosphere corrects itself like you say, it won't mean a thing if no one's around," Waisanen barked. "Genetic integrity first."

"If the embryos are in vacuum cryogenic containers, won't that last for months?" the Frenchman asked.

"If it's a hydrogen Dewar, maybe. Some only last weeks. We must make sure."

"Chicken or egg?" Bill shrugged, looked at Girard, and sighed. "How far to Miami?"

* * * * *

The Port St. Lucie nuclear power plant, one hundred twenty-five miles north of Miami, operated two reactors generating more than one thousand megawatts each. It had weathered the Big Fart superbly. The operators, exposed to the anoxic storm, suffered the same fate as most of humanity and died within moments. Operators in both control rooms had followed protocol and reached for the Safety Control Rods Actuator Mechanisms— SCRAM buttons.

The SCRAM would drop control rods, shutting down the reactions, and allow the cooling systems to carry away the heat of decay. One operator reached the button, the other didn't. He passed-out three feet short, fell, hit his head on the console, and died.

The reactor kept humming along supplying heat, to create steam, to spin turbines, to supply electricity to a world that no longer existed. But, three weeks after the apocalypse, a small coolant leak drew down the reservoir to dangerously low levels and the automatic emergency SCRAM system finally kicked in, launching the spring-loaded control rods within the four-second design window, which stopped subatomic neutrons from striking more neutrons in its usual cascade of radiation, and leaving only the heat of decay. Enough heat to melt steel and vaporize concrete.

The emergency cooling system started, but unfortunately the coolant pumps began cavitating, throwing the pump shafts out of balance until they ground to a halt. The heat of decay then built up, melting through the fuel plates into the containment vessel. The fuel rods burned through five of the six feet of concrete in the bottom of the tower, but the system performed as designed. It stopped the rods a foot short of the outer shell, containing the radiation and preventing a massive release of radioactivity.

If someone were around to pass out safety design awards, the Port St. Lucie engineers would have deserved them. But, they were dead, and no one was there to check on the plant and follow up after a partial core meltdown. No one was there to vent the small but steady amount of hydrogen gas created by the reactions of heat, uranium, steel, and concrete. So, explosive hydrogen gas slowly built up within the tower.

* * * * *

After lunch, Jason and Mark finished morgue detail. Emily surveyed the infirmary's pharmacy, and Terrance searched inmate records in the warden's office. Come late evening, Emily poked her head into the foyer.

"Hey, let's cook a real dinner in the break room."

Terrance yelled from the hallway, "Good idea. Dr. Adams, do the honors. Go flip the circuit breaker for the kitchen."

Jason glanced at the ominous stairs. "Sure."

His lone headlamp fought the darkness of the stairwell. Hiking down the corridor, he thought he heard a noise as he passed Pod Room Seven, making the hairs on his neck stand up.

Jason whispered to himself, "As Mark said, ain't nobody on the whole planet. No way, no how. No way, no how."

Jason entered the mechanical room, found the electrical box and the kitchen circuit breaker.

Switching it on, he turned to the computer to check fuel consumption. As he sat, he smelled something foul. Using his nose, he followed the odor around to the front of the generators.

* * * * *

Reverend Branson heard someone enter the mechanical room. Retreating behind the generator, he quickly opened the knife from the multi-tool. Footsteps approached on the other side. He raised the knife.

* * * * *

Jason stepped between the humming generators and found a potential source—the warden's corpse.

"Oh, it's you. Forgot about you. Don't go anywhere. We'll give you a dignified transfer tomorrow."

Jason turned, marched down the corridor, and back upstairs.

The crew prepared food in the commercial kitchen. More dry goods—soups, spaghetti, and freeze dried. After dinner, they migrated to the warden's office. Jason remembered the man sitting sentinel in the mechanical room. "Hey, I forgot. There's another corpse in the generator room."

Sergeant Davies turned on the warden's computer. "You and Mark."

"Crap!" Mark groused at Terrance, "And, what are you going to do while we haul corpses?"

"I'll look for the admittance records."

"What?" Mark threw his arms in the air. "You get to sit on your ass while Adams and I drag dead people out!"

Sergeant Davies stood and barked, "No matter how informal we've become, that's insubordination. You're under martial law, mister!"

Mark wagged his finger at the sergeant. "Hey, take your martial law and stick it up your ass."

Emily broke in. "Cool it! A little less testosterone, fellas. The corpse can wait till tomorrow." She turned, grabbed Jason by the arm and pushed him into the warden's desk chair. "And, the records, I think this is why we brought a psychologist."

Jason sat and typed while the others looked over his shoulder. "Like I said, the women are all on the bottom, sub-floor nine, just like Pandora's box."

Mark puzzled. "Huh?"

Emily answered, "Greek mythology."

Jason opened the bottom desk drawer. It held a box of cigars and a bottle of scotch. "Zeus gave Pandora a box containing all the evils in the world. She wasn't to open it, but she did."

He took a cigar and set the box on the desk. Mark picked up the scotch, took a swig, and passed the bottle to Emily. Rolling the cigar between his fingers and smelling it, Jason puffed on the unlit cigar.

"And, the evils escaped to plague human-kind. But, 'hope' lay in the bottom of the box and—"

Mark reached for a cigar, but Jason slammed the lid. "Pandora closed it, trapping 'hope' inside." He looked up. "So, humans will always have hope."

No one spoke. What began as light-hearted banter turned quickly to heavy gravitas. The nurse squeezed Jason's arm. "Alright, snap out of it. No pity parties, not in my ward."

The psychologist half smiled and called up the first female prisoner. "A prostitute."

Mark slapped Jason's shoulder and bounced up and down like a little boy. "We got hookers."

Jason continued. "She's bipolar, cut her boyfriend's penis off, then stabbed him twenty-three times."

Mark changed his tone. "Oh, shit. Let's, ahh . . . skip her."

Emily laughed.

Jason clicked to another. "Killed her husband." *Click.* "Killed her husband." *Click.* "Killed her pimp." *Click.* "Killed her dry cleaner."

"Dry cleaner?"

"I don't know. Must have put starch in her panties." Jason read farther. "Six priors, each time off her meds." *Click.* "An embezzler. Hey, they're smart and good with numbers. I'll come back to her."

The bottle passed around. *Click.* "An anarchist."

"She'll fit right in," Emily quipped.

The psychologist continued. "She blew up buildings, but nobody was in them."

The bottle got back to the sergeant. "This may sound dumb, but how do we get them pregnant?

Mark jumped on it. "You see, when a mommy loves a daddy, she lets daddy put his willie in mommy's cabbage patch."

"Shut up!" Davies spat.

Jason paused. "Good question. If we let nature take its course, it may take a while. The colonel was

186

long on what and why, but real short on how." He turned to the sergeant.

"I haven't received orders pertaining to that."

Emily offered, "Can't we get the sperm from the males, while they're still asleep?"

Mark threw up his hands. "Hey, that's where I draw the line, but knock yourself out."

Emily glared at the handyman.

Jason smirked. "She meant get the gametes surgically."

"Hey! I know. We let the whores get the sperm."

Terrance and Jason laughed.

"Why bother." Mark grabbed his groin. "Gunther's stud service right here. No surgery involved. And, the females, don't need to wake them either. I mean, I don't mind."

Emily cringed. "That's so unethical, not to mention sick. How would you like to wake up with—"

Sergeant Davies interrupted. "That's for the colonel to figure out. The hospital compound generators will only support so many. For now, let's revive ten or twelve females and get back to the compound. We can wake more later. Mark, how many could this place support?"

"These are big-ass generators. Five, six hundred or more."

Terrance stepped toward the hall. "Adams, put a list together. We'll start first thing in the morning."

Emily yawned. "Yeah. There are real beds in the infirmary."

Jason stayed seated. "You guys go ahead. I'll work on this a while.

A Hope in Hell

* * * * *

Reverend Branson held the knife in front of his face and whispered, "Until we know where the guards are, stay here, stay quiet." Orange shapes moved in the darkness. Several figures approached.

A big man with tattooed face leaned forward. "What are you gonna' do?"

The reverend put his finger to his lips. "God's work." He eased the door open, closed it behind him, and tiptoed down the hall.

The pale gnarled hands of Reverend Branson rubbed the dust from the window of a sarcophagus. He moved to the next, and then the next . . . he paused. Inside lay a man with a bleeding cross branded on his neck.

"Isaiah, my right hand." Branson typed on the control panel keypad. The read-out displayed: "Revive."

* * * * *

Floridians, used to hurricanes, fled to the false safety of their homes to wait out the tempest. Young and old died in their storm shelters, cellars, bath tubs, under or atop their beds. Few had died on the highways. The ambulance containing the three scientists sped along Interstate 95 with only scattered blockages—trees here and there, but few trucks or cars athwart the road. At the city limits of Port St. Lucie, a major overpass had collapsed. They backtracked to an exit and spent the next two hours picking their way through city streets. Soon enough, they pulled back on the highway toward Miami.

The thick clouds of the Devil's Inversion shortened the period of functional light. Darkness arrived by the time they hit the outskirts of Miami-Dade County. With twelve miles to go, they decided to spend the night and wait for daylight before picking their way through the post-apocalypse debris.

Bill pointed to the gas gauge. "Still got over a half tank of gas. How is the oxygen supply, Carl?"

Waisanen squirmed around and checked the pressure gauges. Three empty tanks, two partials and three fulls."

"Tomorrow, we will need to find a hospital or welding supply store and get some more." Bill wrapped a sleeping bag around him and nestled into the front seat.

His companions laid their bags out in the back of the ambulance.

The biologist looked at a map. "We've cleared the route, so the return trip will be much quicker."

The depressing gray of morning didn't come soon enough for Bill. Used to the comfort of the Mountain, he slept fitfully in the ambulance front seat. When Girard passed him a military coffee pouch, he activated the warmer and gratefully sipped in the caffeine.

Waisanen navigated as Bill exited I-95 and picked his way through the side streets. They stopped several times to backtrack and find alternate routes, but finally pulled up to the

Southern Florida Institute for Reproductive Health. Though built of steel and concrete, the building didn't survive the storm well. A taller building nearby had collapsed, crushing one wing of the clinic, and only half of the roof remained on the other sections. Donning a respirator, their navigator crawled over debris clogging the entrance. The others followed, assuming the biologist knew what to look for.

When Waisanen entered a side room, Girard stuck his head in. "There is no cryo-refrigeration here."

The biologist pawed through shelves of drugs and pulled out a few bottles. "Progesterone, clomid, HCG, ovulation inducing drugs. We may eventually need these."

He filled a satchel of drugs and proceeded down the hall. Many of the side rooms lay so devastated Bill could not have guessed their functions. When they got to the end, Bill noticed nothing special, but Waisanen yelled, "Bunko!"

He clawed at a pile of rubble, passing boards, jagged metal, and broken furniture to Bill. He burrowed into the pile, finally clearing a path to a stainless-steel cylinder, which he dusted off.

"Liquid nitrogen! Even if the electricity is out, this will circulate to the Dewar flasks." He tipped the bottle. "I don't know, feels empty."

He followed the tube until it disappeared inside a metal vault. Bill and Girard helped to clear an area in front, but the vault stood locked. They tried hammers and crowbars, then tried to guess the passcode.

Road Trip

Carl sat down exhausted. "Adenine, cytosine, guanine, and thymine . . . the future of the human species written in a four-letter alphabet—three-and-a-half billion years of evolution, three feet away, and we can't get to it."

Bill raised a finger. "There's a butane torch in the gear. It's worth a try."

He tried it on the door hinge and, after several minutes, the metal turned red, and then white, hot. He and Girard took turns. An hour later, a few hammer blows knocked the door from the hinges. It teetered and crashed to the floor.

Waisanen stepped inside the vault and found several shelves with various-sized vessels. He picked one the size of a large pumpkin, and checked the label.

"Yes! Embryos, fifty-some. It's supposed to be negative-195 degrees. It's already warmed to negative 160, but cold enough. They'll be viable. Eventually, we'll have to hook them up to another cryogenic supply." He pulled out a larger Dewar. "Five hundred in here. Temperature negative 182. Excellent."

Bill helped drag the large bottle out of the vault. "How do we know they're not from axe murderers?"

The biologist nodded. "We need the portfolio data." He rummaged around on a desk and found a computer. He pulled the hard-drive and added it to their pile of loot.

Bill helped load three Dewar tanks and slid in behind the wheel. By two in the afternoon, they exited Miami, and began retracing their route up Highway 95. They made such good progress, the atmospheric scientist no longer resented the biologist's insistence that they retrieve the frozen embryos before working on the satellite communication. In a matter of a mere three hours, they again wove their way through the side streets of St. Lucie.

* * * * *

At three in the morning soft footsteps approached outside the warden's office. Jason slept in front of the computer screen, his head on the desk. *Pat, pat, pat.* The steps drew closer. Jason twitched as if trying to awake. A hand reached out toward him.

* * * * *

Jason dreamed of dark shapes reaching out of the earth. A boy hopped from rock to rock avoiding the menacing reach. He was the boy. He slipped, falling toward the grasping shapes.

He felt a hand on his shoulder.

"Jason. Wake up." Emily shook his shoulder again.

He startled, raising his head and focusing on the face looming over him. "Emily, you scared me."

"Jason, I remember that guy. That guy in the pod room was in the news. I remember because some nurse caught him selling organs on the black market. He was a surgeon, ran a cardiac ward."

"What are you talking about?"

"A heart surgeon. Right here. Doctor Hans Fleischer," Emily almost squealed.

"A heart surgeon in a prison? That's not likely." Jason rubbed his eyes and called up a rap sheet as Emily looked on. He stopped scrolling to read.

"Holy serendipity. Convicted for murder, taking organs from homeless people. Thirty-two-year sentence." Jason snorted. "A health-care reverse Robin Hood, stole kidneys, eyeballs, and ever-loving hearts from the healthy, and sold them to the desperately-ill, but wealthy."

"How do we get him to help?"

Jason looked at the psych report. "I don't know. He had a puritan upbringing. Sexually repressed. Hmm?"

"I'll tell Terrance in the morning." Emily patted him on the back and exited with a smile and a "good night."

Chapter XV

Mail Order Brides, Please

Sergeant Davies hollered from the hallway, "Let's go, sunshine. We've got a whole day of pardons to deliver."

Jason roused slowly, remembering the conversation with Emily about the inmate heart surgeon and felt a weight lift. *Lots of if's, but . . . Hope is the thing with feathers.* He reached in his pocket and took his blood thinners.

Jason entered the office. Terrance, Mark, and Emily, already awake, sipped coffee from labeled mugs. *The mugs must have belonged to the guards.*

Terrance fixed on Jason. "What'cha got, Freud?"

"Nine females who should be able to adjust about as well as anyone. Another thirty or forty who need anti-psychotics."

"Men?" Emily asked.

"Most of the men have long records of violence. But, there's one we need. Well, I need." Jason looked at Emily.

"There's a heart surgeon. A Doctor Fleischer," Emily interjected.

"He might be capable of performing a heart transplant."

As Jason tried to read Terrance, Mark gave a thumbs-up.

"Alright! Awesome, man."

Terrance frowned. "This is above my pay-grade. My orders are to secure and revive assets, female assets. We finish our mission, then talk to the colonel."

Emily jumped in. "But, Jason may not have—"

Jason held up his hand. "The sergeant's right, Emily. Let's get this done and then deal with it. First up is Georgia Barnes, a hooker with a heart of gold. The case psychiatrist said she was a good mother."

"We wake the nine women, get them back to the compound, and then come back." Terrance started toward the stairwell. "Let's move. I'll flip the elevator breaker. You guys get a couple gurneys."

Mark whistled a tune from *The Wizard of Oz*, and turned to Emily. "Gee, Dorothy. After we find Tin Man a heart, maybe we can get some gonads for Sergeant Davies."

"Shut up, Mark," Davies retorted.

* * * * *

Terrance descended the stairs and marched along the second-floor corridor. As he approached the mechanical room . . . *Clink.* He put a hand to his pistol and looked around. Proceeding cautiously, he entered the room. Noticing an almost rancid smell, he looked down the generator aisle.

* * * * *

Mark sat on his tool box in front of the first-floor elevator. Emily and Jason pushed gurneys next to the doors and waited. Impatient, the mechanic stood and repeatedly jabbed the elevator button.

"Anytime, dumb-ass."

Emily's shoulders slumped. "He probably can't find the breaker."

"He couldn't find his ass with both hands in broad daylight. Shit, I'll go." Mark snatched his tool box and turned to the stairs.

Mark again made the long march down the second-floor corridor. "Terrance. Terrance! Where the hell are you?"

He entered the mechanical room, flipped the elevator breaker, and returned to the corridor. *Screech.* Desk legs scraped across the concrete floor. *Clank.* The finality of steel bars closing.

Mark peered down the dark hall. "Terrance? Adams, Em, is that you?" He bent down, pulled the pistol from the tool box, and shined a flashlight along the corridor. "Shit!"

He ran to the electrical box, flicked a whole row of circuit breakers on, and returned to the illuminated hall. Raising his gun, Mark barked, "Hold it! Hold it right there." He aimed. "Let him go. Put him down."

An orange figure flashed in behind Mark. He barely glimpsed a pipe arcing up, then landing with a sickening *thunk.* He slumped to the floor.

* * * * *

The elevator light glowed green. *Ding.* The door opened. Emily and Jason entered with their gurneys. Jason nodded to Emily. "Ninth floor, mail order brides, please."

Emily smiled and pushed a button.

196

He inclined his head to one side. "I understand this store has a good lay-away plan."

Emily shook her head. "Okay, now you really are starting to sound like Mark."

The doors closed and reopened to the illuminated second-floor corridor. Emily frowned. "Why are all the lights on?" They exited and pushed the gurneys thirty feet from the elevator to just outside the mechanical room. "Must have a good reason to waste electricity."

"Mark? Sergeant Davies?" Jason paused over the mechanic's open tool box. *Pistol's missing. What's that on the floor? Blood?* Jason picked a large crescent wrench from the box and whispered forcefully, "Run. Run to the elevator, now."

Emily furrowed her eyebrows as Jason stood up and pushed-dragged her toward the corridor. She staggered, but kept her feet.

"Aarrggg!" Three orange-clad figures charged out from the cover of the generators.

Reverend Branson stepped behind them, brandishing a pistol. "Get them!"

Jason and Emily lurched for the lift as other inmates burst from the side rooms. They stumbled, but dove into the elevator car. Jason bounced to his feet and slapped at the buttons. The doors almost closed, but an inmate's hand intervened. The psychologist swung the wrench, smashing an orange forearm. Emily repeatedly jabbed the "close" button, but a prisoner jammed in a broken length of rebar.

The doors opened. Jason swung again and again. Doors closed . . . An inmate swung a pipe. Doors opened. . .

Reverend Branson stood in the middle of the corridor. "Step back!" He aimed. The inmates parted, the doors almost closed. *Bang!* A bullet pierced the panel, but they closed and the elevator motor whirred.

Emily turned to Jason, white showing around her irises. "What the hell?"

"Inmates. How did they wake up?" Jason finally gathered his wits. "Oh, no! No, no, no! We're going down!"

"Eeek!" Emily reached for the up button, but stopped. "We're trapped."

The indicator flashed sub-floor three . . . four . . . five . . .

She sobbed. "What about Mark and Terrance?"

"The inmates probably think there are guards around. They'll hold them as hostages."

Subfloor eight . . . nine . . . *Errrk.* Cables screeched and darkness enveloped them.

"Jason!"

"Hold on, they cut the power." The psychologist pried the doors apart. His headlamp revealed a thick slab of concrete with a small opening at the top and bottom. "We're between floors."

Flash. The corridor lights lit up.

"Oh, my. That means they're coming."

He forced the opening wider, lay on his belly and slid out, crawling onto subfloor nine. Emily followed as he rushed down the hall.

"We gotta hide."

Passing nothing but an endless series of pod rooms, noise echoed from the far end. The stairwell doors swung in. Jason grabbed Emily and ducked into the nearest room.

She cringed. "Did they see us?" Jason put his ear to the door. Shouts and footsteps came nearer. Emily held her breath as they heard running right outside, and breathed a sigh of relief as the footsteps faded.

"Gaw'd, damn it. They gotta be here somewhere. Search every room." Someone bawled above the general noise.

Bam. Bam. Bam. The sound of doors banging open and closed made Jason tremble.

"Damn it!" He turned to Emily who was already among the pods.

She opened one. "Too big. This one's yours." She opened the next. "Just right." She hurriedly stripped down to her panties.

Jason looked on, bewildered.

"Don't just stand there and stare. Get the coveralls off of Big Bertha. Hurry."

The *bam, bam, bam* continued from the corridor.

Jason jumped to it, removing the orange coverall from the large woman in the opened sarcophagus. Emily slipped into the prison orange jumpsuit retrieved from her pod.

Bam. Bam. Bam. Closer!

She stashed her clothes into the bottom of the box, shoved the sedated inmate down and over and climbed in. "Make room, girlfriend."

Jason finished zipping up his jumpsuit, transferred his nitro pills, and came over. "No matter what happens, stay here, stay quiet."

Bam. Bam. Bam. Very close.

"Close the damn lid and get in the other pod!" Emily snapped.

The psychologist started to lower the lid. . . *Wham!* The door flew open. Three inmates stared at him.

Oh, shit. Palid, sweating, their coveralls half open, blood on their arms, hands. *From their IVs, or from Mark and Terrance?* The three spread out, each wielding a makeshift weapon.

Jason froze. He flashed back to his college days as Hamlet, and turned away from them. "Ah. They's ain't here. I already checked."

"What are you doin' here by yourself?"

Jason kept his back to them. "This 'uns a split-tail, but shit, she's uglier 'n hell." He slammed the lid, spun around and winked. "I swear there's got ta' be some decent-lookin' whores here some'wheres."

Two of the inmates grinned from ear to ear. One with a bleeding crucifix branded on his neck continued staring distrustfully.

They headed out. "Come on, Isaiah. We gotta find those two, or the reverend will throw a fit." The third inmate scowled suspiciously, but went along.

Jason thanked the constant cloud cover for his pale complexion. He could blend in.

He followed them out the door and joined in the search.

* * * * *

The hydrogen within the St. Lucie nuclear power plant containment vessel increased to a high enough concentration to blow up and send the eleven thousand cubic yards of cooling tower concrete and steel over a three-mile radius, shake the earth for thirty miles, and release lethal radiation for sixty. Yet, it sat inertly for lack of a spark. Within the structure, no batteries leaked and nothing moved to provide the trigger for ignition . . . until an overhead iron support beam, weakened by the high heat of radiation decay, failed. One end swung down, striking the concrete floor. Most of its potential energy instantly turned into mechanical force—noise and deformation—but a very tiny amount transformed into friction heat, and that released electrical energy—a tiny. . . electrical . . . spark.

* * * * *

Even through the ambulance's rubber tires, Bill felt the earth move. The noise hit next, a sudden explosive *bang!* The pressure wave struck the vehicle, shattering windows and pushing the car sideways. Bill slammed against his seat restraints, his head snapping hard enough to concuss his brain against the skull. He blacked out for an instant.

When he woke, his head rang, his lungs burned. *Oxygen!* The air bags had deployed, forcing him to wiggle out of his seat to the middle aisle. Girard lay slumped in the passenger seat, moaning, blood on his forehead. *Respirators?*

A Hope in Hell

Thud, thud, thud, bam! Bill stared out at softball-sized pieces of concrete bouncing off the pavement like ice balls in a hailstorm. One hit the hood of the vehicle. *No time.* His lungs yearned for oxygen, he crawled to the back. Waisanen lay on the floor. One of the Dewars had tumbled forward and lay atop him. *My God. Is he dead?*

Bill labored to get oxygen, chest heaving, he desperately searched the jumble for the respirators. Head buzzing . . . senses fading. Fighting off the blackness, he saw one of the large oxygen cylinders and dove for the valve. He turned it. Cupping his hands around the nozzle, he inhaled, his head cleared and strength returned to his arms and legs. He went back to pawing through the gear and found the respirators. He donned one and hurried forward to slip one over Girard. Soon, the French scientist's chest moved and his eyes opened. Bill immediately turned back to Waisanen. *Where do I begin?* He grabbed the top of the big Dewar bottle and rolled it away.

The atmospheric expert cringed. His stomach rebelled, lifting bile into his mouth. *Poor Carl.* He looked away.

Returning to the front, Bill found Girard awake, but frozen in wide-eyed horror. The French scientist pointed out the side window. A huge column of smoke arose from the beach. A single parabolic-shaped tower now stood where there had been two. Bill puzzled for a moment until realization hit. *The nuke plant. Radiation. Oh, shit!*

"Radiation. *Tout de suite.*"

Bill tried to restart the car again. It didn't even sputter. "Carl's dead. I'll find a vehicle." He pointed to the back. "Can you grab an oxygen bottle?"

Girard nodded. Bill exited to search the block, but the only cars on the street appeared totaled. A large department store building stood two blocks away. *Parking garage?* Bill jogged. The overhead garage door stood closed, but damaged panels left a rent. Bill crawled through. The garage sat mostly empty with only a handful of sedans. *Stupid! The drivers are not here, so no keys.* Bill hurriedly looked in each car.

In the seventh one he saw a figure slumped over in the front seat. Yes! He opened the door, searched the lady for a key and found none, but her purse lay on the floor. He grabbed her legs and pulled her out. *The smell.* The scientist tried the start button and the control lights came on. He pulled up to the garage door. No way to activate it. Inching the bumper against the panels, it bent outward. He backed up and rammed it, careful to minimize the impact and not deploy the air bags. The door tore from its tracks and gave way. Bill sped up the street and braked alongside the ambulance. Girard helped wrestle several oxygen bottles into the sedan.

"We must go, now. Get away from the radiation."

Dr. Johnson looked in the back of the ambulance. *The frozen embryos!*

"Monsieur Johnson, we should leave now."

There might not be other opportunities to acquire embryos. Bill wrestled one of the large Dewars out of the ambulance and into the trunk.

Leaving the trunk open, he jumped behind the wheel.

Speeding through the streets of Port St. Lucie, they careened around the post-storm flotsam.

Girard's muffled voice came through his half-mask. "We stay on the respirators until we are at least sixty miles away. We do not know how much, ahh . . . radiation dose we were exposed to. It takes two hours to get sick and throw up." He looked at his watch. "So, we will know in one more hour."

The I-95 on-ramp lay ahead. Bill gunned it. The freeway allowed him to quickly put Port St Lucie miles behind them. Bill looked at the odometer. *Get fifty or sixty miles away. Find water, wash everything down.* He massaged his temples. Headache? Nausea? *But, that may simply be from the percussion of the blast.* His ears still rang.

* * * * *

For fifteen minutes, Jason followed the inmates. *Twenty or so.* In each room, they opened the pods searching for Emily and himself. At the end of the corridor, one of the inmates headed for the stairs. "Enough of this shit. I'm going back up."

The one with the bloody crucifix, the one they called Isaiah, shoved the inmate against the wall and threatened him with a shiv. "The prophet said find them. Everybody search the next floor up."

A husky man with tattoos around the eyes and a length of pipe in his hand challenged Isaiah. "Back off. He's one of mine."

Jason stayed to the rear of the crowd. *Bob the Basher?*

Bob and Isaiah stared at each other. Another inmate intervened.

"Save it for the guards."

The famous assaulter finally pointed his pipe to the stairwell. "Go on. Search the eighth floor."

Again, Jason blended with the mob and pretended to search. An hour later, they reached the end of subfloor eight.

Eventually, Bob lifted his pipe and slashed it through empty air. "The hell with it. Let's get upstairs and talk with that other one. Find out where the hell the guards are."

Jason lagged behind. The strain of climbing seven floors weighed on his chest. *Hell of a time to have an apocalypse.* He felt the nitro pills in his pocket just for reassurance.

The search party returned to the second floor and marched to the mechanical room. Jason recognized Reverend Branson and Dr. Fleischer. The doctor sat at the computer. Four others sat with them.

Isaiah reported the failed search. Reverend Branson, The Prophet, stood on a desk and waved the pistol. "Know ye the might of the Lord. We shall confront our jailers. Mr. Bragga, take your people up the stairs. Isaiah, grab the prisoners, we'll use the elevator."

Jason followed most of the inmates marching down the corridor. He looked back to see Terrance and Mark pulled from one of the side rooms. Two prisoners dragged Mark. Blood matted his hair and stained his coveralls.

Jason thought of what the inmates would find on the first floor, no guards, a world without breathable air, how . . . *The respirators! The only way to leave this prison.* His stomach lurched. Crap, they left them inside the break room. Jason tried to push to the front.

Bob the Basher led the way. He eased the stairwell door open, and peered into the lobby. Pipe in hand, he charged onto the floor with the implement-wielding mob behind him.

Jason made a beeline for the break room. Three convicts followed him. Jason stepped inside, then turned back, pointing down the hall.

"Y'all go search them rooms ahead. I'll take a look here."

The inmates charged past. He quickly rushed in, scooped up the respirators and bottles, wrapped them in a sheet, and stuffed them into a cabinet. The other inmates returned. Jason slammed the cabinet shut and stood up. "What'd you fellers find?"

The inmates stood dumbfounded. "Nothing. There ain't nobody here. No guards, no nothin'."

Jason pretended to finish searching. "Ain't nothing here either. This don't look normal at all. Something's going on."

They returned to the foyer where most of the convicts gathered. Bob looked out the front door. "This makes no sense. There's nobody out there either."

Reverend Branson parted the crowd and examined the weather stripping and duct tape around the front doors. He pointed to two inmates. "Look outside."

The two hesitated, but stepped through as Branson held the door open, and then closed it behind them. They walked out ten paces, looking right and left, but they quickly panicked and turned around. Gasping, the two staggered back to the door.

The Reverend held it shut as the two fell to their knees, chests heaving. "Interesting."

Branson finally swung the door open as others grabbed the two inmates and dragged them inside. They wheezed and coughed.

"Gawd damn! *Cough*. Couldn't breathe."

The second prisoner pointed out. "I saw the guards. A whole pile of them. Dead."

Reverend Branson gazed outside. "What else?"

"A few cars. Stock still. Trees blown down."

Someone from the crowd piped in. "They did it. They blew up the planet."

Others joined in. "They had a war. A nuclear war."

Bob the Basher quelled the crowd. "Shud'up. Nothing's blown up out there. But, ya' can't breathe."

The Prophet turned to the back of the foyer. "Bring forth our jailers."

Jason panicked as two inmates dragged Terrance in front of the crowd. Both had crucifixes tattooed on their necks.

Several in the mob yelled, "Kill them!"

Blood seeped from one side of Terrance's head, but he tried to speak, "The oceans . . ." He choked. "Turned over, carbon dioxide storm . . ."

A Hope in Hell

Reverend Branson looked out the doors, raised his arms, knife in one hand. "God has delivered us from the depths of hell." He turned to the mob. "He has shaken the foundations of the world and punished the descendants of Cain."

Sergeant Davies appealed to the crowd. "The whole planet's dead. Oxygen generators are keeping us alive."

Suddenly five or six acolytes, inmates with crucifixes, bent Terrance backward over a desk, pinning him down. He struggled. "Idiots. The world's gone."

"He wears the uniform of Mammon!" Branson shouted. "God has judged the world and destroyed the old. The blood of the goat shall redeem us in the eyes of the Lord." The knife hovered over the soldier.

Jason panicked and pushed forward, his face flushed. Branson's lips moved, but Jason heard only the pounding of his own irregular heartbeat. *My arms can't move.* He finally screamed, "No!"

Everyone looked at him.

The reverend pointed. "Blasphemer!"

Several arms seized him.

"We need him ta' find out what's—"

Something struck his face.

Branson raised his arms in supplication, his eyes fixed with the force of inner vision. "Oh, Lord. Accept our sacrifice."

He plunged the blade into Davies' chest. Blood spouted. The Prophet looked up in prayer, then pointed to the blasphemer. They forced Jason forward.

"You are either with me or against me."

Branson's knife poised inches from the psychologist's throat.

Bam! Bob the Basher slammed his pipe on the table. "He's one of my gang."

Everyone froze. Half the inmates raised their implements and faced off against those surrounding The Prophet.

Isaiah held up his shiv. "He was in one of the pod rooms by himself."

"I was just lookin' for women. Hell, we better fin' out how we can breathe in here or we're all gonna be dead." Jason's voice shook.

Doctor Fleischer stood off to the side of the confrontation between the gangs. "He ist correct."

Some of the crowd added scattered approval.

Branson waved his hand to the acolytes to let the blasphemer go. "So, be it."

Jason collapsed. The crowd dispersed. Some headed for the kitchen. Dr. Fleischer pointed to Mark who, still unconscious, lay atop another desk.

"Get 'dis man to zee infirmary. We might need him."

Jason furtively fumbled for his nitro pills and slipped one under his tongue.

* * * * *

Emily squirmed inside the cramped sarcophagus. *Jason where are you?* She spoke under her breath. "Damn it, he could be dead. What the hell do I do now?" She started panting. *Don't lose it, girl! Come on, breathe—just like Lamaze class.* She calmed, and exhaled a sigh. *Slap.* The corpse-like pod-mate threw an arm over her. Emily stifled a half scream.

"Shit. Keep it to yourself, sister." She flung the arm away.

* * * * *

Jason followed the men to the infirmary where two inmates hoisted Mark onto a bed. Mark groaned and twitched, but remained unconscious. Dr. Fleischer patiently looked over the equipment, then returned and examined Mark's head.

A din of activity issued from the lobby—hollering, people rushing. Fleischer nodded toward one of the side rooms. "Vee shall take ein x-ray."

Jason helped to move Mark and position him on the table. He tried to stay focused, but his head pounded from taking the nitro.

Other inmates circulated just outside the infirmary. One stuck his head in. "Is he gonna' live? I didn't think I hit him that hard."

Doctor Fleischer ignored him.

Jason turned to the inmate. "What was all tha' hubbub 'bout?"

The young man grinned, "Bob said we could wake some of the women. Most everybody is on the ninth floor."

Jason flushed. *Oh, no. Emily!*

The inmate noticed his reaction. "Don't worry, there's plenty for everyone."

Jason looked at the doctor. "I, ahh . . . gotta' take a leak. Back in a minute."

He grabbed a gurney, exited the infirmary, and stalked to the elevator. None of the orange-attired men stopped him. Jason entered and repeatedly pushed sub-floor nine. The doors closed. The psychologist counted the floors as he descended. *It's taking forever. Emily, hang in there.* The indicator finally came to sub-floor nine. The doors opened.

He could see activity more than halfway down the corridor. *That's about where Emily's hiding!* Jason rushed forward, pushing the gurney. As he got to the commotion, his stomach sank. Men hauled half unconscious females into the corridor. Some inmates raped women in the side rooms. Jason shouted, "Hey, stop! You can't just pull them out. Set the controls to revive and come back tomorrow."

Nearby prisoners stopped and stared.

"Mind your own fucking business."

"Who the hell are you?"

"Screw off. Get your own."

Jason gave up and raced ahead to Emily's pod room. No inmates there, yet. He found the pod, put his hand on the cover and whispered, "Em. Em!"

Thwang. The lid behind him flew open, hitting him in the back of the head.

"Jason." Emily sat up and looked down at Jason nursing a bump on his head.

"What the . . ."

"Sorry. I changed roommates. I didn't get along with Bertha." Emily clambered out of the sarcophagi.

"Shh. They're waking some of the women."

211

Emily grimaced. "Are they . . ."

Jason nodded. "It's off the rails out there. Get on the gurney. Pretend you're asleep." Emily hopped up and he covered her with a sheet.

"What about Terrance and Mark?"

Jason hesitated. "Mark is upstairs, and ahh . . ."

The door swung open. Two inmates poked their heads in. "What we got here? Find a pretty one?"

Jason felt sweat trickle down his back. "Try 'nother room, sailors. This 'uns for the doc'."

One inmate crossed his arms blocking the door. "I mean it. This 'uns a nurse and that doc' feller wants her. Now, let me git 'er upstairs."

The second inmate pulled at the first one. "Come on there's plenty." The one blocking the door gave Jason a scowl, but turned and left. Jason pushed the gurney into the corridor. Inmates removed the sarcophagi liners and used them as pads and blankets. He hurriedly wound his way through a sprawl of liners and female bodies.

Another inmate challenged him. "Where you goin'? Let me see her."

"Stand aside." Jason pressed forward, but the challenger barred his way and reached for the sheet. The psychologist folded his arms and leaned against the wall. "This one's got a rash. You can have her if ya want." The inmate hesitated. Jason pointed at him. "Hey, you like blondes? Busty ones? There a beauty in twenty-seven."

"I'll take a look." The prisoner grunted and stalked off.

Jason kept silent, eyes down, and hustled toward the elevator. As the distance grew between him and the inmates, they lost interest.

Jason closed the elevator doors. "Em, it's okay."

Emily sat up, sobbing, and buried her head in his shoulder. "You said Mark is upstairs, alive? Terrance?"

Jason sadly shook his head. "Didn't make it."

"Why?" Emily hung her head. "And, those poor women."

Jason looked at the passing floors. "Listen up. Mark is in the infirmary with a concussion. Reverend Branson and that Bob guy seem to be in charge."

"What's your plan?"

Jason put his head in his hands. "I'm no Henry the Fifth, but . . ."

"Who?"

"Shakespeare's hero, great strategist. I'll explain later. I hid the respirators. Tonight, when everyone's asleep, we'll get them and sneak out."

Ding. The car arrived on the first floor. Jason held the door-closed button. "Until tonight, I'll hide you in the infirmary."

Jason draped the sheet over her. The elevator opened to several inmates milling around the halls. *Act nonchalant.* He pushed the gurney around them toward the infirmary. *Almost there!*

One of the inmates tapped a three-foot length of angle iron on the floor. "Hey, bub, what you got there? Find yourself some company?"

Though his stomach tightened, he managed a casual shrug. "I thought I was done following orders when I got out of the army. Doc wants this 'un. Hell, somebody always thinks they're the boss."

He continued into the infirmary. As the doors swung shut behind him, Jason looked back. *Please don't follow!* The receiving area stood empty. He pushed into a small storage closet and breathed a sigh.

"Okay, Em."

She sat up. "We're in the infirmary?"

Jason nodded. "Stay here. I'll be back."

"What's the plan?"

"Hide 'til I come get you. I have to check on Mark." Jason returned to the x-ray room where the doctor was giving the unconscious maintenance man an injection.

"How's he doin', Doc'?"

Fleischer looked up. "Ein fracture, no major hemorrhaging. Mit time, he should recover. For now, some'sing to make 'im sleep. By morning, he should be able to talk." The doctor turned to Jason. "Rather long bathroom excursion, Herr . . ."

"Ahh. Adams. Jason Adams. Hell's bells, I checked out the women's floor. It's darn chaos down'ere."

The doctor looked at him suspiciously. "Stay and 'vatch dis one. I vill look at 'im later."

* * * * *

Bill aimed the vehicle off the pavement and drove it through loose sand right to the water's edge. He jumped out, stripped off his clothes, and waded into the two-foot surf. Girard followed and began soaping from head to toe.

No dosimeter, no way to determine the amount of radiation. Have to wait for the illness to kick in. Bill felt a general nausea, but neither he nor the Frenchman had vomited. *Maybe the respirators helped, kept us from inhaling particles.*

The scientists passed the bar back and forth scrubbing vigorously. After scouring their bodies twice with soap and sand, they returned to the vehicle.

Bill relied on adrenalin to fight through the pain and fog of his concussion, but his energy faded during the drive. He found the water refreshing. *What next?*

He finally turned to Girard, realizing he hadn't taken time to check the Frenchmen's nasty head wound, still seeping blood.

"How bad?" Bill reached over and examined his companion.

Girard pointed to his ears and shook his head. Bill just now recognized Girard couldn't hear. The NOAA scientist nodded and pointed to his own ringing ears.

ABC's: airway, breathing, circulation. Need to stop the bleeding. Bill pulled his kit bag from the car, emptied the contents on the sand, and tossed the bag into the surf. He found a t-shirt from the pile and pressed it against the head wound. He showed Girard how to press on it, and gestured for him to lie down.

Bill looked at the car, coated in post explosion dust, and decided it may have absorbed too much radiation. *Oxygen is essential.* He pulled the O₂ bottles out and washed them. Bill looked at the Dewar and hesitated. M*aybe the steel enclosure protected the delicate DNA.* Sliding the large vessel onto the sand, he rolled it into the surf, washed it down and let the waves help roll it back out of the water.

Shouldering a fresh scuba tank, Bill hand signaled to Girard that he would find another car. Afraid to put his radiated clothes back on, he trotted off with bare feet and bare behind to what were once rows of beach houses.

Walking between lines of collapsed bungalows, he searched for a car buried beneath the piles of rubble. *None. Probably vacation homes.* Bill carefully picked his way around broken glass and nail-studded boards. *Should have worn shoes.* Then, something caught his attention, a wheel sticking up from the debris. Bill dug through the pile and uncovered a child's bicycle. He pedaled inland about a mile, smirking at the thought of riding buck naked down the road with a scuba tank, on a stolen kid's bike.

Bill turned onto a street with houses that remained mostly standing. The first house stood empty, but he found clothes in the closet and canned food on the shelves. No car though. He slipped on almost-right-sized pants, shirt, and shoes, and hauled the rest to the curb. *Who would have a car?* Bill searched up and down the street for homes with garages.

He tried the third house, locked. He crawled through a broken window and immediately caught an all too familiar whiff of decay. He entered the garage from the house. A new SUV waited there— an all-electric vehicle, hopefully with enough charge to get them to the Kennedy Space Center.

He searched for an activation key. Nothing in the car, nothing hanging on the garage wall, nothing inside the entry way. Moving to the kitchen, two corpses lay on the floor, an older woman clutched to the breast of an elder man in a final embrace. Tears welled in Bill's eyes. He quickly turned away, walling off his emotions.

He walked backward to search the kitchen drawers. *Yes! Keys.*

Bill went to pick up Girard, the remaining oxygen bottles, and Dewar. *Next order of business— breathing.* The two bottles wouldn't last through the night. The scientist searched a database he had downloaded back at the Colorado complex. Most emergency responders have scuba and oxygen. He located a fire station only five miles away.

* * * * *

Jason waited patiently watching Mark, at the same time, he kept an eye on the storage room across the way where he stashed Emily. Two inmates drifted in and started searching the operating room, picking up knives, scalpels, saws, anything they could turn into weapons. *At least they didn't try the storage closet.* He thought of retrieving the portable respirators, but several inmates lingered inside the break room.

Jason half dozed sitting up until the wall clock showed eleven at night. He walked to the lobby and stepped over a couple of inmates sacked out in the corridor. Others milled around. Up the hall, a light shone from the warden's office. He returned to the infirmary x-ray room and waited stoically.

Around two in the morning, Jason hadn't heard any movement from the lobby for a long while. He tiptoed to the storage closet, squeezed in alongside the gurney, and pulled the sheet off. "Emily? Emily?"

Whap. A cabinet door flew open and hit the psychologist in the back of the head. "Ouch."

"Jason, you alright?" Emily crawled down from her hiding place inside a long wall cabinet.

"Damn, will you stay in one place?"

"Sorry."

"Mark is still unconscious, but I think the inmates are all asleep." Jason stuck his head out, looked around the infirmary, then led the way to the x-ray room.

Emily examined Mark's head. He moaned, but remained asleep. "Has he been given anything?"

"The doctor, the Fleischer guy, took an x-ray. He gave him a sedative and said he'd be good by morning."

Emily looked through a drug storage cabinet, pulling out a bottle and a syringe. "This should get him on his feet." She injected Mark. Leaning against the table, she looked down at the floor and asked Jason. "You can get the respirators?"

"I think so."

218

Her lips tightened. "What can we do for all those women?"

"I'm a psychologist, not a hero." He shook his head. "Once we're back to the compound, we'll get help. Maybe we can trade something, bring fuel as bargaining chip."

Their patient stirred.

Emily whispered, "Mark. Mark, this is Emily."

The maintenance man opened his eyes. "Where am I?"

"Mark, it's Dr. Adams. We're inside the prison."

"Aarrggg! My head hurts. Did I get hit on the head or something?"

Jason whispered, "Shhhh! Quiet. We're still inside the prison."

Mark sat up, but immediately lay back. "Ooh, I'll never touch tequila again. I swear."

Jason passed him a pair of orange coveralls. "I know you're hurting, but put these on." The nurse helped Mark slip into the jumpsuit. He tried to stand, but wobbled.

Emily gave him an arm and he hobbled about the room. "Think you can make it to the vehicle?"

Mark nodded.

She looked at Jason. "Okay, Adams. Let's go." They turned off the light and exited.

* * * * *

As they left, a single red diode glowed within the darkened x-ray room.

Down the hall within the warden's office, an identical red LED glowed on a desk intercom. A

219

gnarled hand reached out and pushed a button. "You are correct, Isaiah. Well done."

A shadowy figure stood. "I told you he acted a little strange."

Chapter XVI

Pandora's Box

Jason stole along the hall and Emily followed with Mark slumped on her arm. The door stood open to the break room. A dozen inmates slept on the floor—all men. Most had removed the linings from the sarcophagi for padding. *The women must be on the ninth, still reviving.* He motioned for Emily to stay and began tiptoeing between the snoring murderers and into the break room. He reached the counter where he had stashed the masks and slowly opened the cabinet. Grabbing the sheet full of respirators, he pulled. *Scrape.*

"Damn you . . ."

Jason froze. His heart leapt into his throat, twisting his head around. Nothing.

"Get away. Armmermm . . ." A prisoner turned over and mumbled.

A sleep talker.

Jason returned to the respirators. Scooping up the entire sheet, he padded back to the hall and nodded Emily toward the lobby. They carefully stepped around a couple of convicts asleep in the corridor. The lobby held most of the inmates. Jason negotiated a sprawl of orange arms and legs, approached the entrance, and stopped. An inmate lay across the doorway. He reached for the handle . . .

Click. The lights came on. The orange figure in front of the doorway jumped up. Isaiah held a shiv in his hand.

Jason swung the bundle of respirators and knocked him backward. He jerked the door open and looked back. Other cult members seized Emily and Mark.

"Leaving us?" The voice resounded off the walls. Isaiah jumped forward and slammed the door. He grasped Jason around the neck and put the shiv to his throat.

Everyone else froze.

Reverend Branson marched across the lobby, parting the crowd. "Ahh, is it Dr. Adams? Dr. Adams is . . . was one of our jailers."

Several inmates shouted, "Kill him!"

Branson took the bundle from Jason, held a respirator above his head and turned to the crowd. "The Lord provideth." He examined the masks and addressed the mob. "Essential. Without these, we would never be able to go outside this . . . prison."

Isaiah pressed the shiv against Jason's neck and looked to the reverend. "Shall I?"

The crowd yelled, urging violence.

Jason managed to choke out, "Stop. Stop or we'll all die."

Branson waved the mob to silence. "Death will come sooner for some than others."

Jason spoke through clenched teeth as the shiv brought forth a trickle of blood. "The old world is dead. The human species faces extinction. What is left of humanity needs you!"

Branson roared like an old-time revivalist. "The world needs us? They put us in a box to die! Now, they need us?" He turned to the psychologist. "How would you control us?" His voice started softly.

"Sedated, caged, drugged into oblivion?" His words crescendoed to a shout. "God has destroyed the old world! There is a new order, and I am His prophet!" He raised his arms. "Do you want to live on their terms or live on your own terms?"

The inmates responded in affirmation.

The reverend smirked. "I think they have made their choice, Dr. Adams. Now, where did you come from? Where is this compound?"

Jason looked back at Emily and Mark. They said nothing.

The reverend's lips turned up into a mocking smile. "We'll get to that later."

Isaiah sneered. "Can I kill him?"

Branson waved him off. "Not yet."

The other gang leader, with a dozen inmates gathered behind him, stepped forward menacingly. He slapped the pipe in his hand. "Hey, I'll bash him."

"Mr. Braga, we need fuel, oxygen, guns." Branson offered the respirators. "With these you can get them." He pointed to Mark. "Take this one. First thing in the morning." He turned to Isaiah. "Lock the other two in the holding cells."

Several of Branson's disciples hustled Jason and Emily down the hall to the infirmary. They shoved them into two adjacent cells. *Clang.* The cult members slammed the doors and turned out the lights.

Jason sat in dread-filled silence. The pit of despair in his stomach became a physical ache. All he managed to say was, "I'm sorry."

"You tried. You did all you could." Emily's voice sounded calm, but resigned.

He attempted to shift from morose to anger, but just couldn't. He sought other thoughts, other threads to occupy his mind, but kept returning to the hopelessness of their plight. He murmured to himself, "'Enterprises of great pitch and moment, With this regard their Currents turn awry . . .'"

"What?"

"In college, I played Hamlet. Had a great . . . a great death scene. Shit!"

"What will they do with us?"

"Branson is psychotic, there's no predicting." Jason stood, glanced at the barred window, and wondered how it had survived the storm. He stepped up on the bed and looked out at the darkness.

"What about the compound? We can't tell them where it is." Emily stifled a cry. "My daughter."

Jason sat on the floor by the bars. Emily sobbed and slid next to him. He reached through and comforted her.

"If only Henry the Fifth were here."

"Henry?"

"King of England, hero of the battle of Agincourt, 'Once more into the breach.' I'm afraid I've always been more of a Hamlet than a Henry."

"And, Hamlet was?"

"'Sicklied o'er with the pale cast of thought.' He was less than dynamic."

* * * * *

Jason woke to gray morning light from the high windows of the holding cells. He remembered not being able to sleep. *Must have drifted off, after all.* Emily lay curled on her bunk sleeping fitfully.

An hour later, noise from the lobby trickled in. Emily awoke. The activity subsided and a couple of hours passed.

Jason hollered at two inmates who wandered in. "Hey, how about some food and water?"

Both inmates grumbled and shuffled off.

Later, a tall blond woman entered the infirmary with a tray of food. Her jumpsuit hung partly open, unzipped enough to reveal ample cleavage. Her eyes darted nervously back at the door.

"Hi, I'm Georgia." Her voice sounded forced, but cheerful. "Those assholes don't think people gotta eat."

Jason stepped forward. "Georgia Barnes?"

"Yes, how did you know?"

"I read your profile. We were going to wake you."

Georgia's face turned ashen. "I heard most everyone out there's dead."

Jason looked her in the eyes and grimly nodded. "I know you had a daughter."

The inmate blinked several times, clearly trying to keep tears at bay. Emily reached through the bars and squeezed her arm.

Georgia sobbed a moment, but her head came up. "I can't think about that right now." She passed the tray to Emily. "You hang in there, honey. I've been around gangs before." She lowered to a whisper, "It's better to be one man's bitch than 'everybody's.' Know what I mean."

Emily nodded. "Thanks."

"I plan to find an alpha male to hook up with." Georgia passed Jason a bowl of stew.

His shaking hands fumbled the bowl and dropped it. He grabbed his left arm, and slumped to the floor.

Emily yelped. "Jason! Jason! Get your pills. Listen to me. Take your . . ."

The psychologist struggled to sit up. He got his pills out and popped one into his mouth. "I'll be alright."

Georgia asked, "What's wrong with him?"

"Georgia," Jason wheezed, "do you think you could, ah . . . get the doctor for me?" He placed his hand over his heart.

"Could you?" Emily pleaded.

"Honey," Georgia unzipped her jumpsuit a little more, "I can get men to do 'bout anything. Be right back."

As soon as Georgia exited, Jason spat out the pill.

Emily furrowed her eyebrows. "What? You faked it?"

Jason shrugged. "Dr. Fleischer seems to hold a lot of sway with some of the inmates. I'd like to get him on our side."

* * * * *

The SUV backed up outside the prison lobby doors. Bob Braga, two other inmates, and Mark exited the vehicle and started unloading gear. They forced Mark to help, even though his hands remained shackled in front, and he still wavered on his feet. Branson waited inside with a dozen of his followers clustered around him. Another fifty inmates, a quarter of them women, slowly gathered behind them until they filled the lobby.

Bob came in with a large box full of portable oxygen bottles and respirators. "The hospital had the oxygen masks." Holding one up, he tossed several into the crowd.

Branson signaled his approval. "Well done."

Two inmates came in carrying a long wooden crate. Bob popped the lid off and took out an assault rifle. The crowd whooped and cheered.

Branson picked one up. "God has been kind."

* * * * *

Dr. Hans Fleischer sat in front of Jason's cell and reached a stethoscope through the bars. "*Nach link wenden* . . . left side." He listened for a moment. "Tsk, tsk. Cardiomyopathy. *Nitch so gut.* In zee old days, you'd have been meine best customer—wealthy, but too old to make zee transplant list."

Georgia stood behind the doctor. "What's he got?"

Emily volunteered. "He needs a heart transplant."

Fleischer stood. "Under different circumstances, I could help, possibly, But," he motioned toward the door, "nothing I can do."

Jason buttoned his shirt. "I understand, but thank you. The world is lucky to still have someone of your skills." He nodded to the buxom blonde. "And, someone like Georgia."

"Survival. We all do vat we haft to." Fleischer bent over to put his instruments away.

"I know you can't help us, but please," Jason motioned the buxom toward the doctor, "watch after Georgia."

The ex-prostitute took the hint and threw her arms around Fleischer. "Thank you so much. I've always admired a man with good hands."

Fleischer stiffened, but accepted the hug. "Ahh. Yur velcomen." He gathered his instruments, and as he exited, Georgia joined him, clinging to his arm.

Bang! Bang! Bang! Ratta-tat-tat! Gunfire resounded through the prison walls.

Jason startled. He quickly climbed back onto his bunk and looked out. Several inmates in respirators fired weapons at targets.

"Wow. Didn't take them long to militarize."

The infirmary door swung open, startling Jason and Emily. Reverend Branson marched in with Isaiah in tow. He set a chair directly facing them, sat, and slowly looked at each, as if deciding their fate.

"When I was a young seminarian, the bishops said I had a lot of promise. They said I could look at a person and see their soul." He turned to Emily. "You are very caring, my child. Social worker, nurse?"

Emily returned a defiant stare. "A nurse."

The reverend nodded her confirmation. "How old is your daughter?"

Emily flinched and reached for the locket around her neck. Branson gave into a sick-sweet smile. "I didn't know, until you reached for the

locket. I assume she is alive, and at this compound."
He put out a hand in supplication. "Tell me, is she
disenchanted, rebellious, a little lost?"

Emily blushed in anger.

Branson shrugged and continued, "Don't worry,
we can help her. We've had great success with
troubled youth. Haven't we Isaiah?"

Isaiah smirked with an evil grin.

Emily burst out, "Leave her alone you son-of-a-
bitch. You'll never find her."

Jason stepped forward as if to run interference.
"How's your health, Reverend? Ever have a heart
attack? Stroke?"

Branson frowned and turned his attention to
Jason. "I thought you'd be more concerned about
my mental state. Have you classified me yet?
Dissociative disorder, borderline delusional?

"You don't fool me with that sacrifice farce.
You're just another murderer."

The reverend pursed his lips. "Unfortunately,
necessary. Nothing binds a crowd to an authority
figure like a sacrifice. I merely suggest that God
wants it," he waved toward the door, "when it's
really the crowd that demands it."

Jason spat out, "You're sick."

"Are you any different? You were going to
control them with drugs. You offer emotion-
numbing pills. I offer hope of salvation. Pills . . .
hope." The Prophet weighed them in his hands.
"There is only room for one new world order. Now,
where is this compound?"

Jason and Emily sat silently.

"Nothing? Well, Isaiah, will you have time to take care of this later?"

Isaiah broke into an evil grin. "My pleasure."

Reverend Branson stood up. "Start with the female."

As Isaiah followed the reverend out, he turned back to Emily. "See ya real soon."

* * * * *

Bill steered around Kennedy Space Center's west gate onto the sandy Florida landscape. The still-intact gate blocked the main entrance, but most of the surrounding security fence lay flat on the ground. He kept the wheels turning and veered back to the roadway. He felt like crap and the Frenchman looked even worse—headache, nausea, but they hadn't thrown up yet. *I haven't eaten all day, maybe that would make me feel better.*

He drove straight for the Launch Command Center. From a distance it looked mostly intact.

"La radar domes. No?" Girard searched as Bill circled the building until they viewed the radome near Launch Site Thirty-Nine. Their hearts sank. The eighty-foot diameter satellite communication dome lay in a mound of its rubble—its broken radar dish rested on its side. Bill stopped the car, got out, and climbed atop the vehicle. He scanned north and south. *No upright satellite communication dishes.* He jumped down, shook his head, and pointed toward the Command Center.

Inside the center, Girard's flashlight found a series of satellite communication stations, their screens as large as a small theater's, but dark as mirrors at midnight. He tried one of the computer's power buttons. Nothing.

Bill tapped his shoulder. "Let's look at the backup generator."

He discovered the emergency power for the command complex consisted of two systems: a massive generator with an empty fuel tank and damaged electrical boards, and a battery bank. The batteries would not have been able to carry the building's entire electrical load, but they could possibly carry a few of the computer systems. Bill located the system's tie-in switch by the main breaker box. He prowled around until he found a tool cabinet, which held a voltage meter. Opening the breaker box, he checked the leads out of the battery system—dead as a rock garden.

"We should have rescued that little standby generator from the ambulance," Bill said to himself as much as to the hearing-impaired French scientist.

Girard pointed to his mouth. "This place must have a lunch room, non?"

Bill finally realized how weak he felt. He and Girard prowled the building and found a small kitchen with a few packets of soup in the cabinets.

After eating, Bill's energy returned. Their radiation exposure must not have been that much. He had energy, and a problem to solve. That allowed him to revel in his element. *Get electricity to the computers, repair a satellite dish, establish communication, then get the data.* Bill wasn't sure what to expect from Girard's theories, but he would love to look at changes in the inversion layer near the equator. That may be enough to answer a simple, but important, question: Will the atmosphere heal itself? Will humans be around next year, decade, or century?

The scientist parked Girard inside the center and told him to rest. He planned to search for some utility building or maintenance shop, hoping to find a portable standby generator.

He drove away from the Control Center, stopped, got out, and scanned the area. Looking back, something hung off the roof—tangled wreckage? *Wait*. He climbed atop the vehicle. More tangled struts, and wires, and . . . solar panels. *Luck be a lady tonight*.

Once again, Bill surged with the thrill of discovery. The stress, the nightmares, the weight of the world disappeared. He was fourteen, entering his first science fair with "The Effect of Cumulus Clouds on High-Frequency Radio Waves." He knew he would win when he realized the teachers had no idea what it was about.

Bill requisitioned a ladder and tool belt from a maintenance garage, climbed the roof, and began scavenging through the rubble. *Must have been over two hundred panels up here.* Using hacksaws and bolt cutters, he scavenged eighteen panels. *This heavy cloud cover is blocking a lot of photons, but this'll be enough to charge the batteries*. Darkness descended by the time Bill mounted all the panels, wired them to a central buss, and ran a cable down the wall and inside the building.

Next, he checked on Girard. The French oceanographer still appeared a little dazed from the head wound. Bill changed the bandage and gave him pain killers from a first-aid kit.

The next morning, Bill finished wiring the solar panels and energized the computer systems. Girard went to work inputting formulas they would need once they restored communication to the satellites. The atmospheric scientist spent the rest of the day pawing through the ruins of the radomes, but found nothing worth salvaging. Building an antenna from scratch would take days, and the pilot would be here tomorrow for pick up. *Would he wait or leave them? Damn it!* He returned to the center.

Girard shrugged. "We will build l'antenne tomorrow. Tonight, we need to relax. Let us find a, ahh. . . restaurant. We must have a good meal."

Bill frowned, but thought of eating dried soup again, and decided to go along.

Girard pointed Bill toward the door. "To the Casbah."

They drove toward the city, searching for a grocery store or restaurant when Girard spotted a Wine Cellar store. "Stop, stop Monsieur. We must have wine to go with dinner."

Inside, Girard poked through a back room and emerged with a half-dozen fine bottles. He opened one and took a sip. "Very good."

Bill's stomach growled.

The Frenchman passed the bottle to Bill and opened a refrigerated display case. He winced at the rancid smell, but pawed around and came out with a moldy brick of cheese. "Monsieur, we have dinner."

They moved outside, sat on the curb, and enjoyed the wine and cheese. The Frenchman pointed to his ears. "My hearing, better today. All we need now is girls and a futbol game."

"No. No futbol, no soccer, real American football." Bill stood and posed in a running-back stance. "And, we need beer, not wine." He scanned along the street for anything resembling a tavern. Across the street, a damaged sign half hung down from the roof of the Spaceport Bar and Grille. "Ah-ha, beer!" Bill shouted.

He marched toward it, looked up, and froze in his tracks. He turned back to Girard and pointed at the roof.

"Le satellite dish. They have a satellite receiver dish!"

He ran into the store. Inside a back room, a ladder led to a roof access. He climbed onto the roof and stared at a ten-foot diameter satellite dish.

* * * * *

"My daughter's there, Jason. Don't tell them where the compound is, no matter what!" Emily said it for the fifth time. Light from the barred windows faded to a forbidding gloom.

Jason knew he would never hold up under pressure, but gave a nod in acquiescence. *Change the subject.* "Maybe other prisoners will come around and be reasonable. Georgia appears willing to help."

Whoosh. The door opened, and Jason jumped. It was Georgia with another tray of food.

Jason let out a sigh. "Georgia."

"How're y'all holdin' up?"

"Thanks to you, we're fine." Jason forced a smile.

Emily came forward and placed her hands on the bars. "Georgia, I have a favor to ask you. You see, my sixteen-year-old daughter is at the compound. If I don't make it, would you—"

Bang! Something struck the door. It slammed inward. Isaiah walked in with Bob the Basher behind him. Isaiah wore a wicked-looking hunting knife on his belt. Bob slapped a bat in his hand and leered at Georgia. "Well, look who's here."

Georgia set the tray down. "Oh, hell." She tried to maneuver around them toward the door, but Bob grabbed her arm. "Stay awhile, sugar. We might as well make this a party."

Georgia struggled. "Let go of me, or I'll give you what I gave my pimp."

Isaiah pulled out a set of keys and unlocked Emily's cell door, while Bob forced Georgia inside. Emily retreated to the far corner. Drawing the hunting knife, Isaiah grinned at her as he, too, stepped in the cell. "The Prophet wants to know where the compound is. You can tell us anytime, but it won't make no difference."

Bob pushed Georgia onto the bed and held her down.

Jason screamed, "Hey, she's got nothing to do with this."

Bob ignored him.

Jason grimaced. "Bob, why you letting the reverend boss you around."

The tattooed goliath turned to look back at the psychologist. "Shuddup."

Georgia twisted away and scurried out of the cell. She paused to look back at Emily. Bob pointed at her with his bat. "Get the hell out."

Georgia scampered to the door. "Sorry, honey, nothing I can do."

Jason looked at Emily, who shook her head, her jaw set in grim determination.

Bob grabbed Emily by the wrist, yanked her down. He moved aside but still pinned her arms to the bed.

Isaiah pointed with his knife. "Now. You're a lot prettier than those revives, got a little color in your cheeks." He bent over Emily and ripped the front of her jump suit open.

Jason squeezed the bars of his cell and mumbled, "I'm sorry." He slammed the bars and yelled, "It's north of here! Three hundred miles. Seattle, Sisters of Mercy Hospital. Now, let her go. I gave you the location. Leave her alone!"

Isaiah pointed his knife at him. "Shut the hell up or I'll come in there and gut ya."

Jason banged the bars again. "Hey, Isaiah, Exodus 20:14. Thou shalt not commit—"

Isaiah smirked and dropped his pants. "The reverend approved this."

"So, rape is okay? Interesting. Why do you admire Reverend Branson so much?" Jason pushed his face against the cell bars. "Let me guess. You never had a daddy, so you latched on to the nearest father figure."

Isaiah's face blushed red. "I said shut the hell up."

"I understand. It's classic homoeroticism. You can't have sex with the father, so you substitute someone he approves of."

Isaiah grabbed his knife and lunged at Jason, who retreated.

Jason shifted his gaze to the other inmate. "That's no worse than Bob there. He follows a whole team of losers. The Boston Red Sox, ha!" Jason stepped closer to the bars. "In psychology, we call it underachieving but, in sports, they just call it choking." He wrapped his hand around his own neck and stuck out his tongue.

Bob glared at him with eyes like rusty razor blades. "Fuck you! I'm coming over there next, pretty boy.

Jason badgered him. "Come on. If you use that bat like the rest of the Red Sox, I've got nothing to worry about."

Bob scooped up his bat and ran at him, bashing the bars as Jason danced back.

Emily scrambled off the bed, snatched the keys from Isaiah's pants, and dashed for the door. The inmate dove after her and grabbed her ankle. She tripped, pulled her foot free, and rolled outside the cell.

Bam! She slammed the cell door closed as Isaiah banged against the bars.

"Bitch!"

Through the bars, Isaiah lunged at her with his knife. Emily sprang out of the way, bent down, scooped up a bowl of soup from the tray Georgia left, and threw it in Isaiah's face. "Bastard."

Jason pointed at the keys. "Hurry!"

Emily unlocked Jason's cell, and they rushed to the exit as Bob bellowed for help. Jason closed the door behind them, and they calmly walked out of the infirmary and into the lobby. Several inmates milling around the foyer area heard the howls for help.

Jason pointed back. "Get the doctor, somebody's hurt."

Some of the inmates moved, but others remained, while Jason and Emily made a beeline for the exit. His heart leapt when he saw several sets of respirators hanging by the doors.

Bob continued bawling.

Someone shouted, "What's going on? Hey, stop them!"

Three inmates stepped across their path to block their escape.

Jason took Emily's arm and turned to the stairwell. "Get to the mechanical room."

Emily scampered along. "What's the plan?

"Shut down the oxygen generators."

Jason charged down the stairwell and ran through the second-floor corridor. They reached the end just as inmates with guns burst onto the floor behind them.

The escapees darted into the mechanical room, but a young Latino inmate stepped out and challenged them.

"Nobody goes in there."

Jason tried to calm his breath. "It's okay. The reverend sent us."

"They told me nobody, and dat means you." The inmate poked Jason's chest.

Emily stepped between them. "Hey, handsome. I could make it worth your while."

The inmate crossed his arms. "Nobody!"

Jason waved Emily aside. "Who?"

"Whad'da you mean who?"

"You didn't get here for knocking over a convenience store. You killed someone, someone you knew."

The Latino began poking Jason again. "Screw you, man."

"Why?"

He shoved Jason against the wall. Jason remained defiant. "Why?"

"He cheated me. Mom—" The inmate raised his fist.

Jason starred directly at him. "And?"

"He was supposed to look after me."

"You killed your brother."

The prisoner continued pinning Jason, but punched the wall. "How the hell do you know? He took my . . ." The noise from the corridor got closer. The inmate demanded, "What the hell is going on?"

Jason spoke, slow but determined. "You took a life, now you owe one. This woman is trying to save her daughter."

The inmate stared at Jason.

"One for one. Take a bathroom break."

"That won't even things up."

"No, but it's a start." Jason glanced down the hall. "Now or never."

The inmate let go and hustled to the elevator. "You won't make it anyway."

Jason frantically opened drawers, found two wrenches, rushed to the oxygen separators and began removing the pressure regulators. He handed Emily a wrench. "Finish this." Jason moved to the second separator. "It's a critical component. We'll bargain our way out."

Varrooom. Jason removed one of the pressure regulators. The drone of the generators lowered in pitch. Emily removed the other one. *Varrooom.* Silence.

Twenty armed inmates arrived at the front of the mechanical room. Several dozen others, many of them women, gathered behind them. Jason stepped out from behind the generators, holding the two glass pressure regulators over his head.

"Pressure regulators. If I drop them, they break, and we all die." Jason scanned the fifteen or more firearms pointed at his chest.

"We'll find another," an inmate spat as he stared down his sights.

Jason shook his head. "Not in time. You'll run out of oxygen in five or six hours." Emily walked up beside him. A few of the inmates inched closer. The psychologist kept his back to the generators, but stood his ground. "We want oxygen masks and a vehicle. I'll leave the regulators."

The gathered inmates expressed their opinions.

"Shoot 'im!"

"Kill him."

"Yeah," one woman agreed.

"No! Let him go."

"Who cares."

Crash.

Jason dropped one of the instruments—its glass tube shattered. He held the last one out like Perseus holding the head of Medusa. The inmates lowered their weapons.

"Not your brother's keeper, Dr. Adams?" Everyone turned to the familiar voice from the back of the crowd. The inmates parted, giving Reverend Branson an avenue. He cocked his head, and graced the escapees with a ruddy glow and a beatific smile. "Dr. Adams is a psychologist." Branson slowly marched forward.

Jason held the regulator even higher. "I mean it!"

The reverend paused only ten feet away.

"Don't come any closer."

Branson addressed the crowd. "He's a scientist. He uses his head and not his heart." The reverend smiled again and snorted. "He thinks a heart is just a pump." He stepped even closer. "But, I'm going to prove it's much more. Right here, right now." Another step. "One hundred-fifty people. Another sixteen hundred still asleep. Women. Hope of the future."

Jason's whole body shook. He scanned the inmates, saw Georgia's pained expression. The reverend stepped next to the psychologist and held out his hands.

Jason grimaced, lowered the regulator, and gave it to the serial killer.

Reverend Branson leaned in and whispered, "Never play poker with a prophet." He held the regulator up. "Congratulations, you have a heart. But, I don't think you'll fit into our new world."

Cult members rushed forward to seize the mutineers.

Hurried footsteps resounded from the hall. Bob the Basher and Isaiah pressed through the throng.

Isaiah's knife flashed. "He tricked us. I'll kill him."

Branson held up his hand. "Not now! Ritual must be observed. Sacrifice him in the morning."

Bob pushed in, shouting. "No! he's mine. I get to bash him."

Reverend Branson nodded. "So be it. Tomorrow at dawn."

* * * * *

Bill and Girard found a truck to transport the ten-foot-diameter satellite dish. Working halfway through the night, they moved it to the command center. They left it on the truck bed and parked it close to the battery bank. Exhausted, they finally plodded to the break room, sealed the door and vents, added oxygen, and slept.

The next morning, Bill slugged down some coffee, donned his respirator, and began wiring the antenna with coaxial cable. He lowered the dish off the truck with ropes, secured it to the tarmac with anchor bolts, and ran a power line to the servo motors that aimed the dish.

Girard finished the task by connecting the coaxial to the computers. He grinned and crossed his fingers as he booted the program. The system searched for the satellites, but found nothing. The NOAA scientist programmed the servo motors to sweep the skies searching for a signal. After three sweeps, he rechecked the connections and added a power boost to the receiver dish.

Around midafternoon, Bill still hadn't found a signal when he heard the whine of a small jet as it circled over the Cape Kennedy tarmac. His gut tightened. *If the pilot insists on leaving right away? Do I stay behind? My wife, kids.* He signaled to Girard and they went outside to meet the aircraft.

He explained the importance of the satellite information, but the pilot, under strict orders to return to Colorado ASAP, insisted on prompt evacuation. He gave Bill and Girard an hour to put their asses in the seats or get left until . . . until maybe forever. They let the pilot load the Dewar of human embryos into the craft by himself, while they took one last stab at the system. Bill manually made another sweep of the sky while Dr. Girard listened for the tell-tale beep of a signal. Bill's head pounded. *I have to know.*

He spoke loudly into Girard's ear, "Dammit! I didn't expect to find the GRACE signal, but we should have found the WorldView-5 satellite. It's in geostationary orbit for Christ-sake."

The pilot entered. "Take off in five."

Bill started to argue, but realized it was useless. *Why is he wearing dark glasses when there's no sun? So, we can't get too personal.* The military man turned toward the door.

Girard frowned, then held up a finger. "We have problem to solve, *non*?" He reached into his personal knapsack and pulled out a bottle of wine. "*Nous devons etre cre'ative.*" The Frenchman popped the cork, drank some, and passed the bottle to Bill.

He refused, but the Frenchman insisted.

Bill took a sip and perked up. "Wow. Good shit."

Girard cocked his head, as if to hear him better, and nodded. *"Oui*, a fifty-four French pinot. *Delicieux*. Probably eight hundred dollars a bottle."

Girard took another sip. "The grapes had to be, ahh . . . stressed. No rain in the spring, then lots in the summer. It occurs along a very narrow band of the Chateau Ponete-Canet region every decade or so."

Bill took the bottle, started to drink, and stopped. The bottle slipped from his grip, bursting on the floor.

"Oh, *Monsieur*! That was Premier Grand Cru—"

Bill jumped up. "You said narrow band! The focal point of a TV satellite is too long, too narrowly focused." Bill ran to the computer and changed the scale for the search pattern.

The pilot returned. "Gentlemen. Time to go. I'm sorry, but I got marching orders direct from the president."

The two scientists stared at the blank screens, waiting.

The pilot grimaced with absolute surety. "The wind is picking up out there. We should go right now. It's now or never." He waited a few seconds, then turned and stalked off. "The hell with you."

Bill typed in a tight search pattern, guessing where the WorldView-5 might be. They anxiously watched as the jury-rigged dish swept the skies.

"Dr. Johnson, you must go. I will stay," Girard offered.

"It would be a waste, you don't have the engineering." Bill pictured himself staying, but flashed on his wife and kids.

Outside, a jet engine came to life.

"And, you do not have the theory. *Monsieur*, you must go." The Frenchman pushed him toward the door.

Bill's heart tore in half. He looked at the door, looked at the computer screen.

Beep, beep, beep.

Whoa. Contact! Girard tuned the dish and scanned the computer screen. WorldView-5 showed a major storm.

Bill shouted, "Where is it? What are we looking at?"

Girard frantically typed. The view changed. "This is directly over us. View approximately five hundred kilometers wide. This is north. To the south, major turbulence. Winds two hundred knots." Girard looked at Bill. "The aircraft should not fly."

Bill heard the sound of the jet receding. *Damn pilot is taxiing*. He ran to the door. *Wham!* The wind swung the door back on its hinges. A gust hit Bill, but he pushed on.

He scuttled to the car, and gunned it toward the jet, now turning for takeoff. Hot exhaust billowed from the engine as the plane accelerated. Bill drove directly into its path.

Screech! The aircraft braked hard and engines reversed.

The pilot launched himself out of the cockpit almost as fast as Bill got out of the car. The aviator screamed over the wind, "Damn you!" He pulled a military sidearm and aimed it. "I have—"

Bill stood twelve feet away and pointed south. "Major storm, coming fast, two-hundred knot winds. You won't make it."

"I have orders." The pilot had to lean into the wind as it buffeted him. He finally turned. The gray ominous skies loomed pitch-black to the south. "You're under martial law. If you're wrong, I'll have you shot."

Bill cupped his hand around his mouth. "Park it in that hanger. I'll follow."

He and the pilot soon reentered the command center, pulled the door tight against the wind, and walked to the console. The pilot still held the gun in his hand.

Bill pleaded with Girard, "Please show the pilot the storm."

The Frenchman didn't respond. He leaned on a table with his back to them.

Bill frowned. "How bad is it?"

Girard turned and held up a new bottle of champagne. Bill stopped and finally looked up at the big screen. "It's . . . it's . . . oh my God!"

The French scientist pointed to the display. "Voilá!" He popped the cork, spraying champagne on Bill and himself. "*Merci mon Dieu*. We are saved."

Bill fumbled for words. "The, the, the . . . We're . . . looking . . ." He faced Girard and smiled. "At the equator?"

Girard nodded. The big screen showed clear oceans and land formations extending thousands of miles along a wide belt.

"The inversion is lifting!" Bill hopped up and down, spun around, and hugged the dumbfounded pilot.

The pilot pushed him away with a grimace. "What does it mean?"

Bill marched to the door, opened it, let the wind whip his clothes and face, turned back to the others, pulled his respirator off and inhaled. He raised his arms, tears came to his eyes. "We can breathe!"

* * * * *

"They know where the compound is." Emily paced in her cell. "What do you think they will do? Anna? Will they . . ."

Jason, back in his own cell, sat slumped over on the bunk. He raised his head to murmur, "I don't know." Jason had nothing left. "I really messed up. I'm sorry."

Swoosh. Womph. Wind battered the cell windows. Emily stood and looked out into the stygian darkness. "I know you had no choice." *Woosh.* "Quite a storm." She climbed down and sat on the floor next to Jason's cell. "Come on, Henry the Fifth, any ideas?"

He continued to stare down and shook his head.

"Before all this, back at the hospital, the nurses knew you, they talked. Said you used to go to the neonatal unit and just watch the babies."

Jason shrugged. "I always wanted children. A family. The whole thing." He raised his eyes dolefully.

Emily smirked, and the psychologist gave a short-lived uptick to the corners of his lips. "We put it off, and off, and then divorce, and then this." He pointed to his heart. "And then, this." He waved his hand as if to cover the whole world. "I always planned to but, like Hamlet, I just waited too long."

"Come here." She held out her hand to him through the bars.

Jason took her hand and sat next to her on the floor.

"Well, you would have made a good father."

He couldn't bring himself to respond.

"Do you still want children?" Emily leaned in. "Jason, before I left the compound, ahh . . . I was going to soldier-up, you know, help repopulate the world."

Jason frowned.

"I started taking a fertility drug. What I'm saying is . . . I would rather have your baby than some psychopath's."

Jason's face remained nonplussed. "Bars. Execution at dawn." He looked down. "I'm not exactly . . . in the mood."

Emily pulled his face close and kissed him, her face sandwiched between the cell bars. "Hey, I'm a nurse. I got this."

Jason didn't respond at first, but she kissed him again, and he found himself kissing her back, fervently.

Emily unzipped the breast of her jumpsuit.

"You're serious." Jason caught his breath and leaned in to capture her mouth with his again.

She reached over and rubbed his groin. They moaned and groped like teens in the back of a '57 Chevy.

He drew back, his chest heaving. "How?"

Emily stood up. "Steel bars can't deter the course of true . . ."

Her jumpsuit fell to the floor as she backed up to the bars.

Chapter XVII

Azazel

A predawn light crept in over the cell windows. Emily slept on her mattress lying on the floor next to Jason's cell. Jason stood on his bunk, looking outside. Leftover wind from last night's storm buffeted the glass. He sat back down in contemplative silence.

Full dawn woke Emily. "You been awake long?"

"Yeah, couldn't sleep." Jason climbed back to look out the window. "Emily, I see some blue sky to the—"

Click.

The room light came on as three inmates entered. A heavy-set internee smirked, "It's time, Freud."

Another unlocked the cell. "I wouldn't want to be in your shoes. Bob the Basher is madder than a sack of badgers."

Jason stayed by the window. The patch of blue sky widened.

"Come on down. Don't make us do this the hard way."

"Sure. I'm coming." But, something caught his eye. *White . . . what is it?* He peered. *An Arctic tern?*

An inmate grabbed his arm and jerked him down. They cuffed his hands behind his back.

"Jason!" Emily's voice rose in pitch.

He spoke calmly, "Hope is the thing with feathers."

One of the inmates pointed to Emily. "What about the girl?"

The heavy-set one barked, "The reverend said everybody has to watch."

The other man unlocked Emily's cell and roughly escorted her out.

The hefty internee slid a respirator over Jason's face and pushed him through the lobby and out the entrance. The entire prison population, nearly two-hundred inmates waited. All eyes peered over their oxygen masks as they hustled the psychologist forward.

At the edge of the crowd, he caught Georgia's gaze. Jason barely made out her words as she clung to Dr. Fleischer's arm. "He helped me. We gotta do something."

Dr. Fleischer looked down at the pistol in his belt, then at the assault rifles held by other inmates, and simply shook his head no.

When the henchman shoved Jason into the center of the mass, a circle formed, and Reverend Branson took him from the burly inmate.

Branson forced Jason to his knees. "Before you, is a servant of mammon. His masters sent this man, not to free you, but to control you. He shall be sacrificed this day."

Cult members raised their weapons and yelled support. Half of the others joined in, but many remained silent. Branson took the pistol from his belt and waved it. "And tomorrow . . . tomorrow we shall deal with his masters."

More inmates joined in.

The reverend looked down at Jason and laid his hands on his head. "Confess your sins upon the goat Azazel."

Jason tried to address the mob. "This is it. Last call. We either treat each other like brothers, like sisters, like family . . . or it's—"

Branson cuffed him in the ear and leaned in. "Still trying to use your head."

Cult members came forward, murmuring and touching the sacrifice as Branson continued. "He who has judged shall be judged. You shall atone befor—"

"Enough already!" Bob Braga stepped out from the crowd, a bat in his hand. "It's my turn."

"Amen!" The reverend backed away.

Cult members raised their weapons and yelled support. Half of the others howled and urged Bob on.

Emily found Mark in the crowd. "What can we do?"

Mark shook his head. "Not much, but . . ."

He pulled a length of pipe from inside his coveralls and tossed it into the circle. *Clang-clank.* It clattered on the pavement. Bob looked up, his lip curled back in a snarl.

Mark yelled, "Cut him loose. Make it a fair fight!"

Georgia hollered from the other side. "Yeah, a fair fight."

Ignoring them, Bob imitated a batter stepping up to the plate. "Boo! Boo! Cut him loose."

More in the crowd joined in. The Basher raised the bat.

A tall man in the crowd pointed a finger. "Chicken! Chicken shit."

Bob stopped and turned his scowl on the crowd. "Who said that?" He scanned the gathering, but no one responded. "I don't care. Free him. It'll all turn out the same."

Two inmates came forward, cut Jason's handcuffs, and retreated.

He stood, rubbing his wrists.

Bob pointed his bat at the pipe, and bawled, "Pick it up. Let's get this over with. Pick it up!"

"Pick it up. Fight!" echoed from the mob.

Jason stared at the pipe, and hesitated. Something clicked inside, detached him from his body, as if he looked down at the scene from above. His breath calmed, the crowd noise faded, time slowed.

Bob stepped closer, threatening.

Jason looked west to the bluing sky and murmured, "*To be or not to be*." He removed his mask—dropped it to the ground.

Bob paused, and the mob went silent.

Jason scanned the crowd.

Mark.

Emily's anguished face.

Reverend Branson's severe countenance.

Cult members, tattooed with crucifixes, grouped together.

Georgia standing by Dr. Fleischer—her eyes focused on the pistol in his belt.

Bob stepped closer.

Jason reached for his throat and fell to his knees.

Bob pointed his bat at his opponent. "Coward!" He hefted the weapon again.

Jason fell prostrate—mouth agape as he gasped. His body twitched, convulsed, and stilled. The mob groaned in disappointment. Bob turned to the crowd, pranced, and raised his bat in victory.

Jason scooped up the pipe as he rolled to his feet. The throng reacted, Bob turned—too late. *Bam!* Jason bashed his head in. The big tattooed man buckled to the ground.

The crowd fell silent, stunned.

Reverend Branson shouted, "Kill him!" He stepped into the circle, pointing his gun at Jason.

Jason cast his eyes on the inmates—Emily, Georgia, Branson. He let the pipe clatter to the pavement. The psychologist raised his arms in a Tai Chi Welcoming-Heaven breath.

"My God. He can breathe! Hey, we can breathe again." an inmate pronounced.

Everyone except Branson removed their respirators.

"I can breathe!"

"We're saved."

Several in the crowd moaned with pleasure, smiled, hugged. Tears streaked faces.

Georgia stepped forward. "Hallelujah."

Reverend Branson bellowed through his respirator, "This makes no difference. He must die."

Jason turned pale as an ache seized his left arm. He clutched it and slipped to his knees.

The reverend towered over him. "That won't work this time." He aimed.

Bang!

Azazel

Branson stopped, turned. Georgia stood with a smoking pistol. The reverend clutched his gut and fell.

Georgia wagged her finger. "I don't know about y'all, but I thought he was a little preachy."

A few cult members raised their assault rifles, but other inmates grabbed and disarmed them. Georgia pointed to the group of Branson followers. "Lock up their sorry asses."

Dr. Fleischer walked over to the inmates holding them. "As she says. Lock zem up."

Emily rushed forward. She fumbled through Jason's pockets as he lay prostrate, found the bottle of pills, and placed one under his tongue.

Georgia bent down. "It's his heart?"

Emily nodded and looked up at the doctor. "Help us."

* * * * *

The infirmary's inadequate operating room needed upgrading. Dr. Fleischer requisitioned specialized equipment from a hospital sixty miles away. The inmates supported his requests. Keeping Jason alive gave purpose to many of the former inmates. Grudging respect toward the sacrificial goat grew to veneration, and became infectious.

Fortunately, Dr. Fleischer, used to working alone, didn't need highly trained staff. After hours of prep, he made a median sternotomy quickly, never intending to close it up. Severing the aorta, left atrium, and vena cava, his blood-stained surgical-gloved hands lifted the heart out of the chest cavity.

"*Krankenschwester*. Nurse."

Emily held out a stainless steel bowl filled with ice, in which the doctor placed the organ.

The doctor covered Reverend Branson's opened torso and head with a sheet. He changed gloves and started work on the next table where a heart-lung machine kept Jason alive.

Chapter XVIII

The Children of Job

One Year Later

Jason cupped his hands, pressed his face against a glass window, and peered inside. Several basinets sat in a queue—some of their occupants remained quiet, some wiggled and cried.

Slap. Something hit Jason in the back of the head.

"Honey, snap out of it."

Jason turned and received a buss from Emily.

Mark marched down the hall, carrying a clipboard and wearing his usual coveralls. "This some kind of a joke?"

"Good morning, Mark." Jason nodded.

"A chicken coop? You want me to build a damn chicken coop."

"CDC has cryogenic embryos. They're flying some chicks in today."

"No shit. Chickens."

"Going to have fresh eggs again, Mark."

The mechanic pointed to his chest. "I get the first three."

Jason nodded. "Sunnyside up."

Emily placed her hand on the doorknob to the nursery. "Are you ready, Henry the Fifth?"

Jason smiled. "Once more into the breach."

Emily swung the door open to the sound of crying babies. She wrinkled her nose. "We know why you're fussy." Picking up an infant, she moved to a changing table. "How are the grandbabies today?" Emily glanced at her daughter who played with two identical tykes on the floor.

"Oh, every morning is just a new day in Disneyland," Anna picked up one of the infants, sat in a rocker and began nursing.

Georgia rocked another baby. "Mornin' boss. When are we going to get the new cribs put together?"

Jason promised, "I'll get Mark right on it." He scooped up another fussy infant and walked to the window, where he paced and cooed:

"Hope" is the thing with feathers
That perches in the soul,
And sings the tune without the words,
And never stops at all,
And sweetest in the gale is heard;
And sore must be the storm
That could abash the little Bird
That kept so many warm.
　　　　　　　—Emily Dickinson

The baby stopped crying and fell asleep.

Jason kissed the baby's forehead and returned it to its crib. "Good night, sweet prince."

The End

Epilogue

Those with curious minds may be interested in a few facts grounding the science behind the story:

The Nyos effect:
In 1986, Lake Nyos in Cameroon, Africa, suddenly released volcanic gases that had built up in the lower layer of the lake. The anoxic gases, mostly carbon dioxide, filled a valley, suffocating 1,700 people, 3,500 head of cattle, and most of the wildlife—birds, mammals, and fish.

Tragedy aside, any hard science-fiction aficionado would look at the data and begin hypothesizing: If a small volcanic lake can store and suddenly release such volumes of gas, what could the Pacific Ring of Fire with hundreds of volcanoes and several super volcanoes, combined with the oceans' vast stores of clathrates (methane and carbon dioxide) do on a planet-wide scale? Though estimates of the oceans' gas volumes vary by orders of magnitude, the volcanic and marine sources together could provide enough mass for a carbon gun, a theoretical worldwide Nyos event.

Additionally, the story utilizes a temperature inversion to hold those gases in the lower atmosphere, which also provides a pathway to return the atmosphere to a breathable state.

The actual cause of deaths at Lake Nyos was hypercapnia, high carbon dioxide levels in the blood. Seven to ten percent CO_2 in the air can increase blood CO_2 levels from 45 mmHg to 75 mmHg, resulting in mental confusion, unconsciousness within two minutes, and death soon after.

I formerly worked as a fish hatchery manager, and we sometimes anesthetized fish (for live spawning) with CO_2. We had to be very careful to not over-expose the fish, or they would not revive.

Genetic diversity:

For biologists, genetic diversity is the yardstick for judging the vitality of wildlife populations. Genes give traits to individuals that lend advantages (or disadvantages) in a given environment. The gene frequencies in established animal populations have optimized over thousands of years, so some parts of the population can survive the vagaries of ecological change. The more diverse a population, the greater the chance a species can survive variable pathogenic and environmental stresses.

Wildlife managers often become concerned when mating populations drop below two hundred pairs. Mathematically, certain alleles would not be carried forward into the next cohort, resulting in less genetic variance and less adaptability. In humans, the eventual result might be physical deformities, behavioral problems, and weakened immune systems.

To avoid inbreeding, the story's post-apocalypse population needed to secure more genetic material: retrieve females from Hell's Gate Sedation Prison, and rescue the vacuum flask "Dewars" containing gametes from the reproductive health clinic.

Sedation prisons:

Most futuristic prisons in science fiction involve cryogenic freezing or suspended animation of some sort for storage of inmates. Of course, internees frozen or suspended through long sentences have no chance for rehabilitation, and suffer no harm other than the world and people they knew would grow old and pass away while they are incarcerated. Science fiction writer Charles Sheffield, in his book, *Borderlands of Science*, proposed a sedation prison, noting the technology is just around the corner, compared with the technological leap required for some type of suspended animation. Additionally, people, in a semi-deep sedated state, age normally, which would be a kind of macabre punishment, but still save on warehousing expenses. Since the setting in *A Hope in Hell* is the near future, the sedation alternative seemed the prime choice.

Internal combustion engines:

The post-apocalypse atmosphere, with higher carbon dioxide levels, lowers the oxygen partial pressure, causing internal combustion engines to take in more air. Instead of the usual 14:1 air-to-fuel mixture, car engines would need to "lean" out the mixture by taking in a larger volume of air. Older cars had carburetors requiring manual adjustment, but modern cars have computers—oxygen sensors in the exhaust provide feedback to a car's fuel injectors to optimize the mix. Of course, electric cars would not have any issues, and jet engines have superchargers—compressed air that would make up for the lower oxygen level.

About the Author

A retired fishery biologist, Darrell Keifer, built a
cabin on the Alaska's Kenai Peninsula and spends
summers fishing. He winters in Arizona where he
writes, hikes, and plays pickleball. Darrell enjoys
writing near-future science fiction grounded in hard
science and narrative anthropology.

Author website: darrellkeifer.net

Made in the
USA
Columbia, SC